PRAISE FOR THE CHUPACARTER SERIES:

"*ChupaCarter* is an uproariously good time, full of humor, heart, and unexpected friendships."
—Zoraida Córdova, award-winning author of *Valentina Salazar Is Not a Monster Hunter*

"A fresh, lively escapade with lots of übercreepy bits. ¡Órale!"
—*Kirkus Reviews*

"Fast-paced and funny, with lively illustrations."
—*The Washington Post*

"Actor/comedian Lopez and Calejo offer a rollicking tale brimming with Latinx folklore and culture about finding one's home in the unlikeliest of places."
—*Publishers Weekly*

"Good and gross humor . . . in this fantasy-infused tale."
—*School Library Journal*

"Lopez and Calejo have created another exciting adventure for young readers that is sprinkled with Spanish words and phrases. The humor in the story is elevated by Gutiérrez's artwork. A great reminder that you can count on your friends to help save the day."
—*Booklist*

"Message-driven but well stocked with chills and chuckles."
—*Kirkus Reviews*

CHUPACARTER
AND THE CURSE OF LA LLORONA

Also by George Lopez and Ryan Calejo

ChupaCarter

ChupaCarter and the Haunted Piñata

ChupaCarter and the Screaming Sombrero

CHUPACARTER

AND THE CURSE OF LA LLORONA

GEORGE LOPEZ

WITH
RYAN CALEJO

ILLUSTRATED BY
SANTY GUTIÉRREZ

VIKING

VIKING

An imprint of Penguin Random House LLC

1745 Broadway, New York, New York 10019

First published in the United States of America by Viking,
an imprint of Penguin Random House LLC, 2025

Copyright © 2025 by George Lopez

Penguin Random House values and supports copyright. Copyright fuels creativity, encourages diverse voices, promotes free speech, and creates a vibrant culture. Thank you for buying an authorized edition of this book and for complying with copyright laws by not reproducing, scanning, or distributing any part of it in any form without permission. You are supporting writers and allowing Penguin Random House to continue to publish books for every reader. Please note that no part of this book may be used or reproduced in any manner for the purpose of training artificial intelligence technologies or systems.

Viking & colophon are registered trademarks of Penguin Random House LLC.
The Penguin colophon is a registered trademark of Penguin Books Limited.

Visit us online at PenguinRandomHouse.com.

Library of Congress Cataloging-in-Publication Data is available.

ISBN 9780593466070 (paperback)

ISBN 9798217042418 (library binding)

1st Printing

Printed in the United States of America

LSCC

Edited by Jenny Bak
Design by Opal Roengchai
Text set in Athelas

This book is a work of fiction. Any references to historical events, real people, or real places are used fictitiously. Other names, characters, places, and events are products of the author's imagination, and any resemblance to actual events or places or persons, living or dead, is entirely coincidental.

The publisher does not have any control over and does not assume any responsibility for author or third-party websites or their content.

The authorized representative in the EU for product safety and compliance is Penguin Random House Ireland, Morrison Chambers, 32 Nassau Street, Dublin D02 YH68, Ireland, https://eu-contact.penguin.ie.

To the moon—thank you for always finding me
—G. L.

To all the ChupaCarter fans out there—thank you!
—R. C.

To my family, who patiently waited countless hours
for me to finish working
—S. G.

CHAPTER 1

Okay, okay, I'm lying.

That's not how it happened.

We weren't supersleuths and we didn't have an office with a view of Albuquerque and a cool bronze plaque.

But you'd be surprised how much trouble a kid from L.A. can get into when his mom sends him to the middle of Nowheresville, New Mexico, to live on his grandparents' farm. He could meet a chupacabra one night while sitting on his roof, moon watching.

They could become best friends. The chupacabra's name could be Carter.

Trust me, it *could* happen...

I know because it happened to me.

My name is Jorge Lopez, and I have a confession to make: my best friend is a seven-foot-tall bloodsucking monster, and ever since my mom sent me away to live a quiet, "normal" life, my life has been anything *but*. Just ask the talking sombrero we teamed up with to find the treasure of El Dorado last month. Or, if you think you're brave enough, have a lollipop and chat with the local haunted piñata. They'll tell you. If exercise is more your thing, go for a run with the killer vampire dogs called the dips... you're guaranteed to get a great workout with them!

Anyway, back to the sleuthing thing.

Like I said, my three best buds and I weren't professional detectives or anything like that. But word about some of the mysteries we'd solved had obviously gotten around, because we finally got our first "official" case.

It happened exactly one week after the last day of school. Liza, Ernie, Carter, and I were hanging out in the woods about a mile from my grandparents' farm on a warm, sunny afternoon, climbing trees and just generally goofing around. After everything we'd been through over the last few months, we were all hoping for a nice, peaceful summer.

Turns out, things were only about to take a turn for the *scary*...

Somewhere behind me, I heard Ernie shriek, "Aaaahhh! A chupacabra!" And Liza and I gave each other looks like, *Uh, you think he just noticed that about Carter now?*

But when we turned and spotted the huge, fur-covered, fang-faced monster—who, by the way, most definitely *wasn't* Carter!—the two of us started sounding an awful lot like our pal Ernie.

The monster waved and said hola, showing us a smiley mouthful of gleaming white fangs, which didn't help us feel any less scared. He politely introduced himself. I think he said his name was Pepe, but it was kind of hard to hear him over our shrieks and screams of panic.

"*Carter! Where's Carter?*" I shouted, looking frantically around for backup.

"¡Ah, sí!" The strange chupacabra grinned. "¿Dónde está Carter?"

Just then, the big guy dropped down from a mass of thick branches overhead, landing as gracefully as a cat right beside me. "Right here!" he said.

But suddenly he froze, his eyes narrowing suspiciously on the other chupacabra. "And I'm right *there*, too . . . ?" I could see the supernova of panic exploding in the brown depths of Carter's enormous eyes. "JORGE, HOW IS DIS POSSIBLE?" he cried.

"Carter, that's *not* you!" Liza tried to explain. "That's another chupacabra!"

At Liza's inarguable logic, the big guy seemed to relax. A fangy grin that would send any goat (and probably most people) running for its life spread across his furry face. "Dat make sense! Hola, Not-Me!"

Pepe the chupacabra waved a skinny, clawed hand in return. "¡Hola, Carter! ¡Es un honor! I've very much been looking forward to meeting you and your amigos!"

"You... you've heard of us?" Ernie asked, sounding more than a little surprised as he peeked cautiously out from over my shoulder.

"¡Cómo no!" said Pepe with a sheepish giggle. "What chupacabra hasn't heard of Carter and his three amigos? You are all muy famosos!"

"Famous for . . . *what*, exactly?" Liza wanted to know.

"*For what?*" Pepe looked at her like she'd just grown a third eyeball. "How about solving el misterio de la haunted piñata? Or finding the lost treasure of El Dorado!" Pepe was beaming at us now, happy as a mosquito at a blood bank. "I have to say, when I heard how the four of you gave all that treasure back to the people, I almost cried."

Whoa. So he really had heard of us. "Who told you about all that stuff?" I said, honestly curious.

Pepe laughed. "Gossip is not only a two-footer thing." I'm assuming "two-footer" was chupacabra slang for humans. "Forest animals talk, too."

"You're saying a little birdie told you?"

"Actually, it was a blue jay," said Pepe. He sounded like he might be telling the truth, too, so I decided not to poke any more fun. "Pajaritos get a nice bird's-eye view of the world and pass along mucha información."

Huh. That kind of made sense when he put it like that. (Note to self: make sure there aren't any birds flying by when you hide Grandma's cooking pot so she can't make her infamous pork stew.)

"Do you live around here?" Liza asked.

Pepe shook his shaggy head. "No. Mi familia y yo live very near the Sierra Pelona mountains."

"Hey, isn't that in Cali?" I said. "Right by Los Angeles?"

Pepe looked impressed. "You know those mountains?"

"Well, not *personally* or anything. But I'm from L.A."

"What are you doing way out here?" Liza asked the grinning chupacabra.

Suddenly that bright, fangy smile froze, dimmed, and fell into a deep, fangless frown. "My clan is in trouble," he revealed in a low voice. He sounded anxious now. Scared. And he looked it, too. "We are about to lose our ancestral home!"

CHAPTER 2

"Why? What happened?" Ernie asked Pepe.

The chupacabra shook his head sadly. "Nada. *Yet.* But I have seen the two-footers with the red vests. They came in great metal beasts with four round legs that spin and spin and spin. They studied our lands closely, all the way around, measuring them with their strange tools."

"You mean, like, surveyors?" said Liza.

"¡Sí! That is the word I heard Grandfather use! They were surveyors!" Now a sort of gloomy hopelessness filled the large, almond eyes. "They are going to destroy our tierra. Our woods. They are going to kill all the plants and animals and build enormous dead structures like the ones on that long road to the north." He was talking about the strip mall on Yucca Street. "The two-footers are coming, because Señor

Gomez can no longer protect us. That is what Abuelo said."

"Who's Señor Gomez?" Carter and I wanted to know.

"Maybe you should start from the beginning," Liza suggested.

Pepe didn't say a word for a good half a minute. He stared down at his giant clawed toes, as if deciding how much he could say without getting into trouble. When he spoke again, his voice was low and secretive. "My grandfather would not like me telling you all of this," he explained slowly. "I had to sneak away even to come here. He doesn't want me to get involved. He believes everything will turn out all right, but I know it won't. My grandfather is the elder of our clan and I do not like to disobey his wishes. The two-footer I told you about, Señor Gomez—he is my grandfather's friend. My grandfather has known him for many moons. He is also called Archie."

Ernie blinked in surprise. "Hold your seahorses. Are you talking about *Archie Gomez*, the famous movie producer?"

Pepe nodded like he thought so but wasn't sure. "I believe so. Señor Gomez makes pictures that *move*.

You can watch them on the talking boxes. I have seen some. They are very funny."

"Oh yeah, they're great!" said Ernie. "He makes some awesome horror movies, too! Like *Dorsal's Revenge!*" His excited eyes flicked to me. "You know, the one with the bottlenose dolphin that gets taken over by an alien parasite and starts eating spring breakers?"

I shook my head. "Nah, I don't watch scary movies. I get enough nightmares just living with my grandma."

"I don't understand," said Liza. "How is that movie producer involved?"

"It is his land we live on," Pepe explained. "He bought it to protect our home long ago."

"So, what happened? He's selling it now?"

"No, they are going to *take* it from him!" Pepe said ominously.

I frowned. "How come?"

"Because Señor Gomez's company is about to *die*."

"To die?" Carter didn't seem to like the sound of that.

"You mean, go bankrupt?" Liza asked Pepe, and the chupacabra nodded in a solemn, hopeless way.

"Sí. That is what Grandfather said."

Liza turned and those sharp brown eyes found mine. "The production company must be in debt.

Probably about to go belly-up, and the debt collectors must've hired surveyors to value his other holdings, which is where Pepe's home comes in. They're going to take it to help pay off his debt, most likely."

It made perfect sense. That had to be what was going on, but... "Uh, how do you think we can help you?" I asked Pepe.

From the pocket of his vest, the chupacabra brought out a crumpled sheet of paper and handed it to me. There were a bunch of words on it. Well, more specifically, jobs. The sorts of jobs you'd find on a movie set. And they were all spelled how they sounded, not how they were actually spelled, which made them kind of hard to read.

CHAPTER 3

"KIDNAPPED?!" Carter's owl eyes bugged like he'd just watched a goat go flying across the smiling face of the moon on a witch's broomstick. "Why dey forcing kids to sleep?"

"Not kidnapped as in kids *napping*," Liza told him. "Kidnapped as in *taking people*. Making them go missing."

"I don't get it. What does this have to do with you?" said Ernie, staring up (and I mean *way* up) at the frowning chupacabra. I wasn't exactly seeing how it all tied together, either.

"It's Señor Gomez's new movie," Pepe tried to explain. "It's the biggest one he ever made. He put all his company's money into it. But the movie is costing him more and more, and he cannot finish it, because somebody keeps kidnapping the two-footers who are helpin' him make it! They've been disappearing in the picture-making place!" I figured he meant the movie studio. "Then nobody ever sees them again and the other two-footers are getting scared, wanting to quit. Señor Gomez is running out of time *and* money."

"And just to be clear, you believe the people who work the jobs you wrote on this piece of paper are going to be the next ones kidnapped?" asked Liza.

Pepe gave his kangaroo-shaped head a few nervous nods.

"But how did you get this list in the first place?"

The chupacabra pointed a long, clawed finger at his bat-like ear. "¡Los oí! I heard them! See, forty moons ago, I snuck over to the picture-making place to see Señor Gomez—to ask if there's anything I can do to help. I went at night, hoping to see him alone, but he was not there. Then I saw another two-footer leaving. He struck me as very strange because he looked like he came from a different time, wearing a very old charro outfit, and he smelled like he was from a very different time, too! So I followed him and soon we reached the woods and he went in. I thought this was quite strange because two-footers do not

usually walk alone in the woods at night. So I kept following him. He walked far, far into the trees and then finally stopped near a wide river between the mountains. I could not get too close because there weren't many trees nearby, but I saw him talking to somebody.

"I could not see who dat somebody was, because a tree was in the way, but the man I followed said those jobs out loud, reading them from a paper. Then he handed over the paper and said, 'Here's the list. Their faces are by the names, and those are the dates and times I want it done. Follow this list to a tee.' Then, two moons later, the cinematographer goes missing! Nobody's seen 'im! Then, a few moons later, the production designer is missing! Then the music supervisor and the choreographer, just like I overheard! In the same order, too. Look at the list!"

I peeked over Liza's shoulder at Pepe's list again.

SINUHMUHTAAGRUHFR

PRUHDUHKSHN DUHZAINR

MYOOZIK SOOPRVAIZR

KAWREEAAGRUHFR

SKREEN RAITR

AKTOR
STUHNTMAN
PRUHDOOSR

Liza was studying the list, too. "So the first four are the ones who went missing after you overhead all this?"

"¡Sí!" said Pepe. "That's how I know I heard right!"

"But . . . we're not exactly professional detectives," Ernie pointed out.

"Yeah, why don't you go to the police?" I told Pepe. Only, the moment I said it, I realized just how silly of an idea that was. How could he go to the police? He was a chupacabra.

"The police are looking for the missing two-footers, but they'll never find them," Pepe said defeatedly.

"How come?"

The chupacabra shrugged. "Because the ghost got them."

"Hold up. There's a ghost involved?" Ernie was looking between Carter, Liza, and me like he'd spotted a rattlesnake in his bowl of breakfast cereal. "Like, a *legit* ghost?"

"These are the rumors we hear," Pepe told him. "Señor Gomez told my grandpa that some of the two-footers working on the picture say they seen it. They say it's the kidnapper."

Man. Kidnappings, ghost sightings, and a clan of chupacabras on the verge of losing their ancestral home? Talk about some heavy stuff...

"¿Nos puedes ayudar? Can you help us solve this mystery?" There was a sudden spark of hope in the chupacabra's eyes, voice, and his entire furry face, really.

You could still feel the awful stress the poor guy was under, thinking that he and his family and all his neighbors were about to lose their home. I knew what that felt like. I'd lost my "home" more than a couple of times. And it never got any easier. And it *always* hurt.

I'd help Pepe any way I could. "What do you want us to do?" I asked. "¿Cómo podemos ayudarte?"

"Come back with me to Los Angeles!" he said excitedly. "You can stay with us. I will make a nest for you! Help us figure out who is kidnapping the movie people and help me stop them. This way, the movie can be completed, Señor Gomez will keep his land, and our woods can be saved!"

The four of us looked at one another in tense silence. "L.A. is far," Ernie said.

"Yeah, just traveling there means we'd be gone for days," I agreed.

Liza was shaking her head, her voice grim. "My dad would never let me go."

"Neither would my dad," said Ernie. "*Or* my mom."

I sighed, looking up at the big guy. "And neither would my grandparents."

Carter was nodding, slowly, sadly. He knew Pepe had basically asked for the impossible. "I could go," he said gloomily. "But I can't help much alone."

I watched our words stab Pepe straight through the heart. It was like seeing a flower begin to wilt just before it withers and dies. It was terrible.

Finally, Liza turned to him again. Her face was a mask of pity. "I—I don't think we can go back with you," she told him. "It's just not possible. We're just kids."

Pepe gave it one last shot. His huge, pleading eyes slid slowly to mine as he whispered, "¡Por favor! Están seguros?"

Honestly, I'd never wanted to say yes to someone so badly in my whole life. I would've given anything to be able to help the dude out. But I knew there was nothing we could do.

So I gave him the bad news. "There's just no way, Pepe . . . They're not going to let us go. And even if we snuck away, one call from any of our parents and grandparents, and the police will be dragging us back within the day."

"I couldn't put my dad through that," Liza said. "Thinking I'd run away."

"I couldn't do that to my parents, either," said Ernie.

"Well, I *could* do that to my grandma," I admitted. "But I don't want her flinging empanadas at me again. I still have a big old chichón on my head from the last time."

As the sun began to set gold and red behind the rows of tall trees, I watched Pepe's eyes dim and his furry face fall. I'd seen popped balloons that looked cheerier than he did. No joke, I felt like we'd just kicked a sad puppy. It was one of the worst feelings in the world.

CHAPTER 4

"Man, I really feel sorry for Pepe," Ernie told me when we were talking on the phone early the next afternoon, both of us on our way to Liza's. "He seemed so helpless."

"I feel super bad for him, too," I admitted. Truth was, Carter and I had basically spent all night talking about him and his situation, trying to figure out if there was anything we could do to help the guy. But, no surprise, we hadn't come up with much.

"I hope Pepe's grandfather is right," Ernie said, "and everything works out okay."

"Maybe it will."

"Hopefully. Are you almost at Liza's?"

"Yeah, me and the big guy are like two minutes away. Maybe we'll get there before the summer is over if Carter will stop chasing *every single squirrel* he sees."

We were all heading over to Liza's to play a little Mouse Trap. Liza was a total board game nerd and that was a pretty good one. Even Carter liked it.

Only, when the big guy and I finally made it to Liza's house, and then into her room, I didn't see any mice or traps. Liza was playing a different kind of game. She was sitting at her desk with a map of Los Angeles County pulled up on her laptop and scans of old *L.A. Times* articles spread out in front of her like a paper explosion.

She didn't even give us a chance to act surprised. "Pepe was right!" she shouted, spinning around in her chair to face us. I stared at her like, *Are you kidding me right now?* But Liza wasn't having it. "Oh, c'mon, Jorge! None of us can stop thinking about this case since we met Pepe. And you *know* you felt horrible when we turned him down."

Well, she wasn't wrong about that. I did have a soft spot for those giant bloodsuckers.

She shoved a printout of a newspaper article into my hand. Uncrumpling it, I saw that it was dated today, and the headline read: THE MYSTERY OF THE

VANISHING CREW DEEPENS. The article was about the mysterious disappearances of cast and crew on the set of Mr. Gomez's new movie. The same news Pepe had come to see us about.

In the article, the reporter talked about how the case wasn't getting much attention because people and the police seemed to think it was nothing more than a fake ploy for media coverage. The article mentioned a bunch of people we'd seen on Pepe's list, and described how they'd just up and vanished.

"See that name below the crossed-out ones?" Liza asked me.

I shrugged. "What about it?"

"That's the screenwriter for Mr. Gomez's movie *and* the next target on Pepe's list! And apparently, he just got kidnapped!"

I carefully reread the last few sentences to make sure I hadn't missed anything. "Liza, all it says here is that the screenwriter had promised to talk to this reporter about the case a few days ago, and last night when they were supposed to meet, he never showed up and now she can't reach him."

"Because he probably got kidnapped!" She looked at me, her eyes big and intense behind the rims of her glasses. "Something really weird is going on in that studio, Jorge...*really* weird."

"Hey, what happened to Mouse Trap?" Ernie said as he came in.

"Forget Mouse Trap," I told him. "Liza's playing Sherlock Holmes instead."

I handed Ernie the article and watched his eyes bug as he read it. "Is this from today?"

"Uh-huh." Liza nodded, typing up a storm on her keyboard. "I've been searching some online archives to see if there've been any other weird disappearances on that studio lot in the last couple of years, but I haven't seen anything yet."

While Liza did her Sherlock thing, I pawed through the mess of papers on her desk until I found one that looked kind of interesting. It was a packet she'd stapled together with the entire cast and crew of Mr. Gomez's movie, their names, jobs, and dates of birth. Liza had used a red marker to circle all the names of the people who were on Pepe's list.

"What is that?" Ernie asked, pointing at the packet in my hands.

"Just some basic info on the cast and crew I've been compiling," Liza said. "I circled all the people on Pepe's list to organize our case."

"Liza, it's not *our* case," I reminded her. "We already told Pepe we couldn't help."

I flipped to the second page of the packet. All the people Pepe thought were in line to get kidnapped were on that page. Curious, I glanced through the names.

> ~~Jane Robby (age 52): cinematographer~~
> ~~Miguel Morales (age 28): production designer~~
> ~~Karin Michelle (age 43): music supervisor~~
> ~~Constance Rodriguez (age 31): choreographer~~
> Robert Villegas (age 55): screenwriter
> Eduardo Cruz (age 35): lead actor
> Manny Martinez (age 33): stuntman
> Archie Gomez (age 62): producer

Then my eyes focused on the second-to-last circled name, and my jaw dropped so far in shock that it nearly disconnected from my face!

"*No way...*"

Ernie glanced at me. "What did you find, Jorge?"

The world seemed to tilt underneath me and I nearly dropped the packet. "It can't be..." I breathed.

"What can't be?" asked Carter as he waddled over, his brown eyes dark with concern.

So I told him: "I—I think the stuntman is... *my dad*."

CHAPTER 5

"Jorge, are you sure?" Liza asked me.

"I— No," I admitted. "But that's his name. Manny

Martinez. My mom told me once. I remember because his name rhymes with 'fanny.' She said it was the only thing she liked about him."

"Manny Martinez is not exactly an uncommon name, though."

"No, but he's the right age *and* lives in L.A."

Swiveling back around in her chair, Liza opened a new tab on her browser. After a minute she said, "There are fourteen Manny Martinezes living in L.A. I can probably find pictures of them online."

"That's not going to help," I said. "I've never seen him."

"Maybe he looks like you."

"Maybe." And suddenly my stomach was twisting up inside of me worse than a deep-fried churro. No idea why, either. What did I care if I looked like him or not?

A few clicks later, the search engine formally known as Liza told us the results: "Not finding too many headshots."

I shrugged, telling myself how much I didn't care. "No surprise. He ran out on my mom and me. He probably ran out on the internet, too."

"Jorge, we have to warn him!" Ernie shouted.

"What? No way. He's a big boy. He can take care of himself."

"But we have to, Jorge!" said Carter. "He's your . . . *papá*."

"We can't." Liza sighed. "We can't warn *anybody* on the list. Think about it. If some villain really is kidnapping people on set, and we warn anyone and the villain gets wind of it, all they're going to do is switch to new targets, and just like that, Pepe and his clan will lose their only chance of finding out who's behind it and saving their home. That list is their only advantage over the kidnapper at the moment. We can't spoil that."

"Then what are we going to do?" cried Ernie. "Just let Jorge's dad get kidnapped?!"

"Yeah, let him get kidnapped!" I said, surprised by the sudden rush of anger that had flared up inside of me.

Ernie looked shocked. "Jorge, you don't mean that."

"Of course I mean it! He left me, didn't he? Didn't care what happened to me or my mom. Why should I care about what happens to him?"

Now Carter looked shocked. "But, Jorge, he's *familia*."

"Not to me," I said, crossing my arms angrily over my chest. "He's never given a rat's behind about me, and now it's my turn to return the favor. Wacha!"

CHAPTER 6

I was a pretty good actor. I'd managed to put on a pretty tough face in front of my friends. But the only person I hadn't *ever* been able to fool was myself. And I knew that deep down inside I *did* care about what happened to Manny Martinez. As much as it annoyed me to admit it.

Seeing his name on Pepe's next-to-be-kidnapped list had hit me like a steaming hot bowl of sopa de tortilla right to the face. It'd left me anxious and fearful and, most of all, confused.

I mean, he might not have been the *best* dad ever. In fact, he hadn't been one at all. But blood was blood, and I felt like I owed him *some*thing. Even if that was only a quick email letting him know to watch his espalda. Problem was, who would believe an email like that?

I could try to find his number and call him up, but he'd probably think it was some kind of prank. He'd never take me seriously. Not one person on that list would. And that's what made this whole situation so tricky. I had no idea what to do. Fortunately for me, good friends will always have your back. And I had some of the best friends anybody could ask for.

I was digging around in the fridge early the next afternoon, searching for a snack for Carter and me, when the kitchen phone rang.

"If it's the government calling, you haven't seen me in a month!" Paz shouted from the living room where she was watching a telenovela. "You heard me? *A month!*"

Trying to ignore the fact that my grandma was giving off some *serious* fugitive vibes, I answered the phone. It wasn't Uncle Sam. It was Liza.

"Hey, why aren't you answering your phone?" she asked me.

I sighed. "The battery's dead. Carter's been playing *Minecraft* on it all morning."

"Well, anyway, it's *on*," Liza said, making my eyebrows scrunch up into a big question mark.

"What's on?"

"No time to explain. Just go with it, okay?"

"Just go with *what*?"

A pause. Then: "Is your grandma home?"

"My grandma? Yeah, she's watching a novela."

"Perfect."

Before I could say another word—*click*—the line went dead.

What the—? I had maybe two minutes to wonder if Liza and my grandma had teamed up in some kind of illegal scheme, then there was a knock at the front door and the doorbell dinged. With a loud sigh, my abuelo pushed himself off the couch and went over and opened the door. And who did I see? Liza and Ernie, both grinning suspiciously and holding some printed sheets of paper in their hands. They both said hello to my grandpa and came on in.

Without even giving me a hint what they were up to, Liza and Ernie strolled over to Paz's side of the couch and asked me, "So, have you told your grandmother yet?"

I thought fast. "Huh? Uh, no. Not yet. I mean..." I said, rubbing the back of my head.

"What's the problem, Jorge?" said Paz. "Cat got your tongue?"

I glared at Liza as if to say, *I don't know what we're doing! Help me out!* "I guess it must've slipped my mind," I told my grandma, not knowing what else to say.

"Kinda hard for me to believe *anything* could slip out of a head as big as yours," said my oh-so-sweet granny without taking her eyes off the TV. "That thing's probably a steel trap!"

Man, the stuff I have to put up with. "Uh, Liza, why don't *you* tell her?"

"No, why don't I *guess*," said Paz. "You flunked one

of your classes and you're starting summer school next week? I saw that coming a mile away."

"Grandma! I didn't flunk anything! And why do you have to be so negative all the time? Why can't you think that the surprise was that they're letting me skip a grade, or something good?"

"Ha! *You* skip an entire grade level?" My grandma burst out laughing. "You should be a comedian!"

"It's actually not about school, Mrs. Lopez," Liza told her.

Paz shooed her out of the way; the commercial break was over and her novela was starting up again. "Well, whatever it is, the answer's no."

What a surprise. With my grandma, everything was no. "But, Grandma, you don't even know what it is!" I shouted. And how could she? *I* didn't even know what it was yet!

"Yeah, but I know what it's *not*," she clapped back. Then, flinging me a nasty sideways glare from the couch, she said, "Why you cryin', huh?"

"I'm *not* crying!" Though, I'll admit I had gotten a *teensy* bit misty-eyed. But that's only because she was so *epically* frustrating!

"Mrs. Lopez, it's about the summer camp Ernie

and I are going to," Liza said. "Camp Treetop. We were both hoping Jorge could attend, too. I have the flyer right here."

She handed Paz a sheet of paper. My grandma looked sort of caught off guard. And she wasn't the only one.

"Camp Treetop's the best!" Ernie told her with a big cheery grin, clearly in full-on salesman mode. "We'll get to camp out in nature, sleep under the stars, and there's this huge waterslide on the lake—it's the biggest in three counties!"

My abuela glanced down at the flyer, then made una mueca like she'd just bitten into the world's sourest lemon. Shaking her head, she handed the flyer back to Liza.

"We Lopezes don't do summer camp," she said. "But if Jorge really wants to sleep under the stars, I'll drag his mattress out into the backyard. And for the waterslide, I can bring down that big blue tarp off the roof and run the hose over it. It's the Latino Slip 'N Slide."

"Here's the price sheet," Liza said, bravely pressing on. "It's really a great value, Mrs. Lopez."

My grandma wouldn't even look at the paper. "I'm sorry. It's too much."

"You don't even know how much it is!" I shouted.

"ANY PRICE is too much!" she shouted back.

"But I'll probably learn a bunch of new stuff there! And you can't put a price on learning!" Yeah, that was me actually getting mad over a make-believe summer camp. What can I say? My grandma just knows how to push my buttons.

"Learning! ¡Estás loco! *Learning!* That's a waste of time! Everything you need to know, you learned in kindergarten! And imagine if all that fancy *learning* makes your head any bigger. We'll have to grease your ears every time you want to walk in or out the front door!"

"Mrs. Lopez, I really want Jorge to come," Ernie said. "I even convinced my parents to pay for his spot."

My abuela's hand flew up like a traffic cop working a busy intersection. She didn't want to hear it.

"We Lopezes *never* accept charity!" she snapped, and you could practically see the last of Liza's and Ernie's hopes shredded to confetti. But Paz wasn't finished talking. "*Except* . . . if it gets Jorge out of my hair for a while. Truth is, the kid's cramping my style."

"Cramping your style? *What* style?!" I yelled.

"How much is it?" Ignoring me, Paz snatched the price sheet from Liza's hand. "Only three hundred dollars? That's a bargain! I would've paid double that to get rid of Jorge for two whole weeks!"

CHAPTER 7

The plan was simple. We'd use part of the money Liza's and Ernie's parents had paid to "Camp Treetop" to buy bus tickets to L.A. Then we'd use the rest for food, hotel, and taxi fare over to Pepe's once we got there.

The only tricky part: finding a suitcase big enough to hide Carter in, since we figured he'd draw less attention that way.

When that idea crashed and burned like an earth-bound meteor, we switched gears and decided to give Carter the old "celebrity in disguise" look.

It was a fifteen-hour bus ride from Boca Falls, New Mexico, to Los Angeles, California, and Liza, Ernie, and I sweated during every last second of it.

I kept having this horrible vision of someone realizing what Carter was, yelling "MONSTER!" then bringing out the pitchforks and torches.

It was probably the biggest downside of having a legendary bloodsucking monstruo as a best friend. You worried about the guy. *A lot.*

The bus finally reached Union Station in Los Angeles and let us out not too far from Gloria Molina Grand Park. I hopped down onto the familiar gray sidewalk, breathed in the familiar L.A. air, and heard all the familiar L.A. sounds—the hum of cars and motorbikes, the wild roar of 747s out by the airport. I felt the power and energy of the Pacific Ocean not fifteen miles to the west.

I knew I was home.

It was almost like stepping into an old photograph, a memory—only there wasn't anything *old* about it. Los Angeles was just as alive and vibrant as the day I'd left.

Man, it's good to be home again! I thought, looking up and down the rows of Mexican fan palms. Nothing had changed!

Only that wasn't exactly true ...

Things *had* changed. I'd changed a little. But most of all, *my family* had changed. It had grown to include three new faces—one of which happened to be *particularly* furry.

I couldn't explain how cool it was to have Liza, Ernie, and Carter with me in the city where I'd grown up. It was as if all the puzzle pieces of my heart had finally clicked into place. And it was better than I could have dreamed.

Standing there on Alameda Street, with Dodger Stadium ahead of us and the Hollywood Walk of Fame only a few miles away, I realized that I was in the same city as my mom again. Probably not even thirty miles apart now. And suddenly, I was missing her so bad it hurt. But I had to keep my head in the game. For now, anyway.

CHAPTER 8

We knew Pepe and his clan lived somewhere on Señor Gomez's ninety acres of private woodland nestled pretty close to the Sierra Pelona mountains.

The mountains were a pretty well-known spot to Angelenos, about seven hundred thousand pristine acres of protected pines.

And firs.

And yucca plants.

And wild blooming flowers.

And over two hundred species of wildlife.

Including bobcats.

Bears.

Mule deer.

Quail.

California mountain lions.

Kangaroo rats.

Hawks.
Ground squirrels.
Eagles.
Toads.
Owls.
And even some bighorn sheep.

Our Uber arrived a few minutes after lunch, and on the drive over, I felt like one of the tour guides on the double-decker buses that tour you around L.A. visiting famous spots. Ernie kept asking me if I knew where Captain Kirk lived, so I pointed at some random house along the way just to give the kid a thrill, and you should've seen how excited he got. I thought he was going to bust through the window with his face, he had it pressed up against the glass so hard. Anyway, the driver found Señor Gomez's property pretty easily, but there was only a mailbox, no house, and a whooole lot of land.

Carter began making these weird high-pitched howls as we started up one of the overgrown trails into the woods, but I didn't think that was going to help much.

"It's going to take us *forever* to find Pepe in there!" Ernie shouted, basically reading my mind.

There probably hadn't been a gathering of bloodsuckers this big since Dracula celebrated his one thousandth birthday back in ole Transylvania.

Fortunately, they were all just as friendly as we'd hoped. Well, at least after Pepe introduced us to all his friends and fam. We shook so many hands—er, hairy paws—I felt like I was running for president or something.

A little while later, Pepe quietly pulled me aside to ask if we'd come to help him solve the kidnapped two-footers mystery. When I told him that we had, the chupacabra came within a fang tip of bursting into tears, he was that grateful. Pepe reminded me not to tell his abuelo the reason for our visit, then got all of us together and took us down to see the guy. And when I say "down," I mean *down* down—maybe twenty yards into a humongous underground burrow that looked like a warren for gigantic rabbits!

Pepe's grandpa, whose name was Carlos, turned out to be a cool guy. He was super stoked to meet us, and he had us all sit around inside his nest and asked us all sorts of questions about ourselves and our trip over. He also asked the big guy about his family, and when Carter told him what had happened and how they'd gotten separated that night, Carlos promised he would find Carter's mother and siblings for him. I'd never seen Carter so excited.

Of course, when Carlos got to the big question, "¿Y qué hacen aquí?" we had to lie to the guy. But he seemed to buy our "visiting some friends and family" excuse, so it was all good. Anyway, after we said our goodbyes to Pepe's grandpa, it was party time.

And let me tell you a little secret I learned: nobody—and I mean *nobody*—parties harder than chupacabras! How was it, you ask? It was like the world's largest petting zoo, the world's biggest luau, carnival, and Cirque du Soleil, all rolled into one!

The food was out of this world, too! I'd never seen a spread like it in my entire life! There was goat stew, goat sausage, goat eyeball ravioli, goat guts ceviche, goat liver pâté, fried goat, grilled goat, goat à la mode, goat tongue sandwiches—and that was just their goat selection.

After the party, the chupacabras held this big ceremony for us, which was supposedly a huge deal among the fanged and furry. It was called the Fanging, and it started with Pepe giving me, Liza, and Ernie chupacabra costumes to wear—fur-covered animal skins and sets of fake fangs. Then the entire clan led us deep underground into their most sacred burrow, which looked like the biggest hobbit hole you've ever seen. There, the elder of the clan, Pepe's grandfather, sat on a huge throne-like chair of twigs, and we all knelt before him in our costumes while the rest of the chupacabras cheered and clapped. Then Carlos touched us all on the shoulders, back, and kneecaps with what I had to guess was the leg bone of a T. rex.

"You are officially chupacabras now!" Pepe told us when it was all over. "You are part of our familia!" Carter was so touched by the whole thing I was pretty sure I saw him wiping a tear from the corner of his owl eyes. You'd think we'd just been knighted by the queen or something.

"Awesome!" shouted Ernie through a mouthful of fangs. "I've always wanted brothers and sisters!"

"Now you have about ten thousand of them," laughed Liza. "And they're furry, too."

"One question," I said to Pepe. "These are fake fangs we have in our mouths, right?"

"Oh, no, definitely not fake! They are all real chupacabra teeth!" he said proudly. "The ones you have in your mouth are my abuelo's. They fell out many moons ago. But he was happy to let you use them for the ceremony!"

His grandfather's old teeth. ¡Híjole! "B-b-but you at least washed these things before I put them in my mouth, right?"

Pepe frowned, looking as confused as a dog at a rainbow-watching party. "Washed them with what?"

Beside him, an ancient-looking chupacabra gave

me a smile that was all withered gums from ear to ear. And that was right about when I nearly refunded all the goat stew I'd recently gobbled down. "Never mind," I told him. "It's been a total horror—I mean, *honor*..."

Surprisingly, Pepe said they still had one more treat in store for us that night. I just hoped this one didn't involve putting anyone else's rotten old teeth in my mouth. We followed him up a set of steps that wound around the massive mossy trunk of a ginormous fir tree. Up, up, up ... into the COOLEST tree house on the planet!

Pepe had even set up an old-school antenna TV for us. Sure, it probably only caught two channels, but it was still a super-thoughtful thing to do.

There was only one problem I could see with the place...

"Uh, where's the bathroom?" I asked, looking curiously around.

Liza pointed over to the clump of leafy bushes where Ernie was currently sprawled out and grinning from ear to ear. "What do you think those are for?" she said with a giggle.

"Wait. I thought this was the chupacabra version of a beanbag chair!" shouted Ernie, leaping to his feet.

"Think again." Liza pointed up at the dark wood ceiling beams. "Chupacabras sleep like bats, remember?"

The corners of Ernie's mouth pulled into a deep frown as he glanced disappointedly back at the bushes. "I thought they smelled kind of funny..."

"This is just like a real summer camp!" I shouted, sticking my head out the window into the cool evening air. Truth was, I'd always wanted to go to camp. At the beginning of every new school year, I'd hear kids talking about how much fun they had at camp and how they couldn't wait to go back next year. But my mom could never afford to send me to one. In fact, the closest I'd ever gotten to camping at all was when my mom would let me set up a sheet tent in the living room. Not that those weren't cool, too. They were. But this . . . *this* was something else!

CHAPTER 9

Later that night, the giant furry nocturnal bat we all referred to as Carter gripped my shoulder and shook me until I sat up with a start, my heart rattling like a maraca in my chest. For un segundo there, I didn't have the *slightest* clue where we were.

Oh right, a chupacabra tree house. "Dude, what's wrong?" I hissed.

"Nothin'. Jess wonderin' what you dreaming about."

"*Say what?*" I whisper-snapped. Now, don't get me wrong. I wasn't anywhere near as shocked as I might've sounded. Chupacabras don't sleep at night. They are nocturnal, and this certainly wasn't the first time Carter had ever woken me up in the middle of my z's for some totally ridiculous reason. What shocked me was that Carter had just violated my recently instituted "most important rule ever, ever, *ever*": NEVER WAKE ME UP TO ASK WHAT I WAS DREAMING ABOUT! It was no golden rule, but still pretty important when you had a buddy with less-than-usual sleep habits.

"Carter, did you seriously already forget our new rule?"

"No..." he admitted sheepishly.

"Then what's the problem?!" I asked. *And it better be good.* In the bunk above, I could hear Ernie snoring his lawn mower snore. *Si no es uno, es el otro.*

"Is no problem, Jorge. I'm jess so excited I wanted to talk to you!" And Señor Fangs looked it, too. I'd seen little kids opening Christmas presents who looked less amped.

I tried to rub some of the sleep out of my eyes. "Talk to me about what?"

"Mi *familia*, Jorge! Carlos said he gonna find dem! I'm gonna see my mamá again!"

I sighed. I guess I couldn't blame the guy. I mean, who wouldn't be excited about finding their lost mother and siblings? "Carter, about that. I don't want you to get your hopes up too high, okay? I'm sure Carlos is really good at finding people, and I'm sure he's going to try his best, but let's just see what happens before you get too stoked."

Carter's face was a picture-perfect confused emoji (plus the fur and foot-long fangs, of course). "But why, Jorge? Carlos already said so."

"Yeah, dude, I know Carlos said so. But what if—what if he can't?"

"Oh, but he can! Carlos said so!"

"Okay, but let's just say he *can't*. Then what? Then you're going to be crushed. Trust me. I know all about getting your hopes dashed. When I was five, my grandma promised to take me to Disneyland one of these years for my birthday. And every year I was *positive* that this was going to be the year. Seven years later and I still haven't even so much as sniffed the *parking lots* at Disneyland. You get me?"

Carter didn't seem to get me.

"All I'm saying is that I don't want you to be hurt," I tried to explain.

"Is okay, Jorge. I won't be hurt. I know Carlos gonna find dem!"

Oh man. This just wasn't the conversation I wanted to be having with my best bud. And it was especially terrible since I was 99 percent sure I knew

what had happened to his family. It didn't take a Sherlock Holmes to figure it out.

The night they'd been separated, Carter and his familia had been on the run from a pack of dips—rabid, bloodsucking vampire dogs.

Seconds from being caught, Carter's mom told him to flee in one direction while she ran the opposite way with his baby siblings so that those evil monstruos wouldn't be able to catch them all.

Carter had gotten away.

You do the math.

Looking up at those huge, brown, honest eyes so full of hope and excitement was almost breaking my heart. It was too much for me to handle right then, so I just said, "Yeah, dude. I've got a feeling he just might find them, too..."

CHAPTER 10

"Rise and shine, sleepyheads," Liza said, waking us up early the next morning.

"Liza, what time is it?" I yawned, sitting up.

"Time to get to work." Liza was tapping her watch impatiently. "We've got a case to crack."

"Mom, I need a few more minutes of sleep," grumbled Ernie, turning over under his sheets. "I don't mind being late to school today."

Liza gave him a funny look as I said to her, "And how exactly do you plan on cracking that case? Because if you haven't worked that part out yet,

I'm going to hit the snooze button and you can wake me when you do."

I actually thought that might buy me some more z's, but then Liza said, "There's no snooze button, Jorge," and grabbed me by the leg, dragging me out of the bunk.

Then she rolled Ernie out of bed, and even though he landed on the floor of the tree house with a loud *plunk!* it didn't seem to help much. The kid was still off in Neverland, counting sheep. "It's time to get up and get ready."

"You still haven't told us the plan," I said, going over to poke the big guy awake.

"The plan is simple." Liza unzipped her travel bag and brought out a stack of files. "I did a little extra research on Mr. Gomez's production company and the strength of his balance sheet. It was already pretty weak, because of a few weird distribution snafus and some odd accounting oversights. Then he went all in on this movie, and with the delays plus the skyrocketing production costs, he's in a terrible spot. For me, it's clear as day: sabotage."

"Sabotage?" mumbled Ernie. Looked like Snorlax was finally coming around.

"It's the only logical explanation. Remember, Pepe followed someone leaving the studio. That was the person with the list of the people they wanted kidnapped. So putting two and two together, it's pretty obvious that person is trying to tank this movie. It's an inside job. Their motive is impossible to say at the moment, so we're going to have to sniff around the set, ask questions, and draw up a list of possible suspects. I don't see any other way to catch this saboteur."

I mean, it was a pretty good plan. Most of Liza's plans usually were. That's why she was the brains of the outfit. But there was just one teeny, *tiny* problem with this particular plan...

"And how exactly are we supposed to 'sniff around'?" I asked. "I think it's going to take more than a smile to get into any studio lot." The big guy grinned at me. "Especially Carter's smile." That one would probably get us run out of town with garlic and wooden stakes.

"Fair point," Liza said with a sly smirk. "But I don't think crew members would have much problem getting in."

"Yeah, but we're not crew members!" Ernie pointed out.

"Liza, if your plan is to get us hired by Mr. Gomez's company so we can get on set, then you could've let us sleep in for the next *month*! You know how long it probably takes to get hired by a production company, especially when you're *twelve*?"

Liza shrugged. "Nope. All I know is we're already hired."

I blinked, shocked. "Seriously?"

"It wasn't that hard, actually. Mr. Gomez's movie is losing crew every day. People are quitting because they're vanishing or scared, so he's pretty desperate for help. Especially for summer interns who they don't have to pay. I took care of all this before we left."

¡Órale! Liza really was a genius!

"Here are your studio badges," she said, digging them out of her bag and handing them out. They were super nice, too. Laminated, with our names, and attached to a handy lanyard so we could wear them around our necks. The badge also showed the movie title: *The Curse of La Llorona*.

"*Hooollld* up!" I said to Liza. "Hold waaaay up.

Why does this thing say the movie is called *The Curse of La Llorona*?"

Liza looked at me like I was one bell pepper short of a fajita. "Because that's the name of the movie."

Last night, Liza had told us Mr. Gomez's movie was coincidentally about a cast and crew that begins to mysteriously vanish while filming a horror movie. "You never said *anything* about La Llorona!"

"So?"

I felt my eyes bug, cartoon-style. "*SO?* People are vanishing on a movie set that's making *a movie* about people vanishing on a movie set."

"Uh-huh. And?"

"And in that movie, it's probably La Llorona kidnapping those people, right?"

"I still don't see your point."

"My point is that this whole thing just feels super wrong! And by 'super wrong,' I mean *dangerous*!"

Liza sighed. "Jorge, please don't tell me you're still scared of little-kid ghost stories."

"Little-kid ghost stories? Do you even know who this lady is?!" I didn't think any of them did, so I broke it down for them like a fraction. "Her name translates to 'the Crying Woman,' and she's one of the most well-known scary stories in all Latino folklore! She's the spirit of a lady who was cursed to spend the rest of eternity wandering around near rivers and lakes, searching for her two children—who, by the way, she'd DROWNED!"

"I'm not liking the sound of this . . ." Ernie said nervously.

"You shouldn't!" I told him. "Because it's no heartwarming tale. But she's the reason abuelitas all over the world warn their grandkids about going near bodies of water at night!" Though my abuelita never actually did warn me about that. She always said it was perfectly safe, any time of day. But I knew it was because she was just *hoping* I'd run right into the scariest ghost this side of anywhere, so she could spend the rest of her life laughing her heinie off about it.

"Jorge, what does La Llorona have to do with our case?" Liza wanted to know.

"Maybe nothing," I said. Then, in my best scary-campfire-story voice: "Or maybe *everything*..."

Ernie and the big guy exchanged panicked glances. "I want my mommy," E-dog squeaked.

"It's just the title of the movie, okay?" Liza shook her head, smacking us with her eyeballs. "Take a chill pill and let's get ready to go. We don't want to be late on our first day."

"Fine! But if La Llorona kidnaps us, you better *believe* I'm going to tell my grandma whose idea this was. And I'm telling Ernie's parents, too!"

"You do that," Liza said, dumping the contents of her suitcase on the bed. "Just please make sure you don't lose those badges. I don't have duplicates."

"I don't get a badge?" asked Carter, sounding sort of sad.

"We're going into a movie studio," Ernie told him. "I think you're going to have to sit this one out, bud."

"Not so fast," Liza said, finding and tossing a badge

to Carter, who caught it happily. "Sabotage means there's a villain on set. A kidnapper. We're going to need protection if and when we catch them. Carter's going to pretend to be your emotional support animal."

"Are you messing right now?" I asked Liza. I mean, I'd heard of emotional support *Chihuahuas*. But a seven-foot-tall bloodsucker? It just seemed like he'd cause everybody else plenty of emotional *distress*.

Reaching into the pile, Liza whipped out a brand-new dog collar. "Carter's playing the role of your four-legged friend. You two are the bright-eyed and enthusiastic summer interns. Everybody know their role?"

Looks like Liza's playing the role of director, I thought to myself.

CHAPTER 11

The Multiversal Studios complex, where Mr. Gomez's new movie was being filmed, was located on the iconic Warner Boulevard in Burbank. According to the info brochure Liza had printed out, it was a sprawling thirty-acre studio lot that had once been America's largest goat pasture. (Carter was super excited to hear this.) There were exactly twenty-two separate filming stages on the property and enough 35mm film to circumnavigate the earth about 150 times.

The uniformed guard in the security kiosk at the entrance waved our Uber through after we showed her our badges, then we were in, rolling along between the rows of airplane-hangar-size stages, the bright morning sunlight slanting down over the sloped aluminum roofs. I'm not going to lie, I was pretty stoked to be there. You could almost feel that movie magic in the air. Ever since I was little, I'd always wanted to take one of those studio tours I saw advertised all over newspapers and magazines in L.A. Only that was just another thing my mom hadn't really been able to afford. It was tough growing up without a lot of dough, because you always see all these kids doing all the things you wish you could do but can't. If I'd learned anything, though, it's that having money or the best clothes or the newest phone can't truly make you happy. That's what friends and family are for. That's real happiness. I'd also realized that if you just wait long enough, and hold on to those little dreams, you'll get to do all the things you wished you could—and *more*. I mean, check it out: I was getting a studio tour. And for free!

Ernie, being the movie geek he was, had his face smooshed up against the window, and was breathing so hard in his excitement that you could see his mouth exhaust condensing white on the glass.

"We *have* to go see the *Star Trek* set!" he said excitedly. "It's only four blocks that way. I saw this behind-the-scenes special once and I think I can get us there just going off memory!"

Liza and I gave each other *Oh brother* looks. "This

isn't a Trekkie convention, Ernie," she told him. "We're here on business. *Serious* business. We don't have any time to waste."

Ernie looked at her like she was a seagull who had snatched away his last lollipop. "But can't business wait until after we've said hi to the Starfleet crew?"

Liza's answer, in case you couldn't guess it, was a resounding *no*.

We moved on, this time accidentally through a movie set, but it definitely wasn't *Star Trek*.

"My bad!" I tugged on the leash. "Carter, get over here!" I hissed.

The big guy reluctantly came over on all fours. "But dere a flock of goats over dere!"

"Carter, you already *had* breakfast!"

"But not lunch," he pointed out.

"Of course not lunch. It's nine a.m.! And those goats aren't for eating! They're actors!"

Liza had this big fake smile plastered on her face, but out of the corner of her mouth she growled, "Carter, you're going to get us thrown out and we've barely been *in*! Now behave!"

As it turned out, there had been a little mistake with the directions the production company had emailed Liza. Mr. Gomez's movie was actually being filmed in Stage 21, not 12.

It was maybe a ten-block walk in the hot Southern California sun, but that was hardly the worst part. The worst part, as we made our way over between the soundstages, was the two cops in patrol blues flying around the corner toward us, maybe half a block up ahead!

¡Santo cielo! They're coming for us! I thought as they came charging our way, shouting into walkie-talkies.

They must've realized that we were just here to gumshoe it up!

No joke, I was about two shakes of a chupacabra's tail from bolting for San Bernardino when the cops suddenly ducked out of sight into a stage that looked suspiciously like the set for my abuela's favorite telenovela. With my heart still trying to thump its way through my rib cage, I watched some guy in a headset hand them each a pair of dark sunglasses and a fat shooting script. Translation: They weren't your friendly neighborhood law enforcement. They were actors, just like the goats.

I glanced over at Ernie to make sure he hadn't colored his undies. By the look on his face, it had been a pretty close call.

Things got better after that. On the next block over, a 1920s gangster relaxing on a plastic lawn chair tipped his fedora to us. A minute later, a storm trooper came hustling over to ask us if we'd seen a Chihuahua in a ballerina costume. Then, as we turned left by Stage 18, a beautiful fairy princess riding a huge white caballo down the middle of the street smiled at us and waved a glittery pink wand. No, hold up.

That wasn't just some fairy princess. That was Selena Gomez!

"*Please* let me ask for her autograph," I begged Liza. "That was SELENA, yo!"

But I'll let you guess her answer.

CHAPTER 12

Eventually, we found our way to Stage 21. But what we couldn't seem to find was anybody who looked like the director inside the enormous twenty-thousand-foot soundstage.

"May I help you?" said a voice.

We turned to see a tall, red-haired lady holding a clipboard.

"Hello," said Liza with a friendly smile, "we're the new summer interns."

The lady looked pretty excited to see us. "Oh, wonderful! I've been looking forward to meeting you three. My name's Lola. I'm the second assistant director."

We all smiled and gave little waves.

"I see you've all got your badges on, that's good. Keep those in plain sight at all times, so security won't bother you. And I see you've brought along your emotional support animal!" Then, getting a good look at Carter: "What an . . . interesting-looking . . . *dog*?"

"Uh-huh! He's a really unusual mix!" I told her with my most toothy grin. *A mix between Count Dracula and a bigfoot, that is.* (I said that last part inside my cabeza.)

Lola seemed to buy that. "That's nice." Then, under her breath, she said, "And you'll need *all* the emotional support you can get interning in this studio."

"What was that?" asked Liza.

"Oh, nothing. Just admiring your courage."

Ernie blinked. "Our courage?"

"If not courage, then definitely *spunk*! And I admire all of it! And I'm thankful for it, too! By the way, have any of you ever interned on a movie set before?" she wanted to know.

When we all shook our heads (Carter included), Lola said, "You're going to have a great time! It's a lot of fun. You'll get to meet all sorts of interesting people, including the director, though you won't see him today. Maybe not even all week. The script's in the middle of a rewrite, so there won't be any filming today, and he probably won't come out of his trailer, either. That's where he usually works. The man is an incredible talent."

Her eyes flicked down to her clipboard. "Anyhoo, I have your call sheets with your departments right here. Okay, so first up is Liza." Liza waved and she handed her a sheet of paper. "You're with art. And which one of you is Ernie?" E-dog politely raised his hand. "Okay, so that's for you. You'll be helping out the camera team. And you must be Jorge." I smiled. *That's me.* "Here you go. You're with the stunt department. That's a fun job! Just *a tad* more dangerous than what your friends will be doing. But let's not kid ourselves, 'safe' is a relative term on this set..."

"What exactly do you mean by that?" Liza asked, but Lola sort of brushed off her question with a "Well, you know how things are nowadays," and handed me the last sheet of paper.

A moment later, Carter said, "What about me?" and I felt my stomach plummet into my toes! Liza and Ernie, meanwhile, tried to hide their panicking faces behind their call sheets.

Lola shook her head, looking confusedly around. "Who said that?"

"Uh, I did!" I shouted.

"I just told you that you were with the stunt department, didn't I?"

"Oh, yeah. Forgot." Man, that chupacabra and his big mouth... I'm not sure my cheeks could've felt more on fire if I dumped a truckload of jalapeños into my mouth!

Lola gave me a strange look. I countered with my most innocent smile. I think it worked.

"All right," she said, glancing down at her clipboard again. "Well, now that you know your roles, find your department heads and let's get to it! We got a busy day ahead of us."

She wasn't kidding. Working on a movie set was kind of like being a worker bee in a busy beehive. Everyone in this place was constantly buzzing around and it always seemed like there was something for them to do. The enormous indoor stage was divided up more than a Danny Boy's pepperoni pizza, and I counted at least five unique sets just waiting to be filmed.

My call sheet had come with a mini map of the place, so it was pretty easy to find my way to the stunt department area. I found a roster on the wall by the bathrooms, and it showed only five names, two of whom weren't working today. One of the no-shows was my maybe-dad.

What else was new, right? The funny part was, up until that point, I hadn't realized just how anxious I'd been about the possibility of running into the guy today. I was pretty good at not thinking about things that made me feel all jittery inside when I didn't want to. But now that I was here, and now that I knew that he *wasn't*, I felt this bizarro blend of relief and disappointment.

Man, being a human can be so confusing sometimes. Being a chupacabra seems a lot easier. And speaking of the giant bloodsuckers, the one whose leash I was currently holding had begun to drag me toward what looked like a set of oversize monkey bars in the corner.

I had to drag him back. "Hey, you can't climb monkey bars. Remember?" I hissed.

Carter gave me a fangy frown. "Course I can, Jorge! I play on dem all da time!"

"No, you don't! 'Cause *dogs* can't grab the bars! They don't have opposable thumbs!"

The big guy looked super confused. Just ten minutes on set and he'd already totally dropped character! What a fabulous actor he'd make...

Anyway, I had just opened my mouth to remind the walking vampire bat that he was supposed to be acting like my loyal emotional support pooch when someone tapped me on the shoulder. I could've easily shrieked my head off in surprise, if I wasn't such a cool Chicano.

Behind me was a pimply-faced guy somewhere in his twenties maybe.

"You're Jorge, right?" he asked me.

"Uh, yeah. How'd you know?"

"I'm good with faces." He showed me a mouthful of braces. "Just kiddin'. They told me you were coming. Lola did. The name's Emmet. You'll be helping me out."

"Oh, cool. Nice to meet you. You're a stuntman?" He didn't really strike me as the type, but I hadn't exactly met many stuntmen.

"Nah. Only helping out. I'm on the audio team." He proudly held up something that looked like an old-fashioned reel-to-reel tape recorder. "I'm the sound mixer. But you gotta wear many hats when you're losing crew like this. I'm sure you've heard about what's been happening, no? About the ghost?"

Bingo! It sounded like the audio guy might have some inside info for me. My heart was thrumming with excitement, but I kept my expression all *GQ* while I frowned and said, "A ghost? Seriously?"

Emmet looked sort of surprised. "You didn't know?"

I shook my head innocently.

He leaned in so close I could smell his perfume. It smelled a lot like Lola's. "You wanna hear a secret?"

"Uh-huh."

His voice went real low as he whispered, "I've *heard* it! The ghost!"

CHAPTER 13

Okay, now we were getting somewhere...

"Oh yeah?"

"Yeah! See, this was about two weeks ago. I was working late in the audio room, running some tape through my Nagra III"—he lovingly patted the portable recorder with his free hand—"when suddenly, the temperature in the room plunged a good *fifty degrees*! Just like that!"

"Was somebody messing with the thermostat?" I said.

"No, see, that's what I thought, too! But come to find out, there wasn't another *living soul* in the entire studio! Well, besides Karin Michelle, the music supervisor on set. But we'll get to her soon enough. Anyway, that's when I spotted the tendrils of *ghostly vapor* sliding in under the door..."

"Otherworldly mist?" Okay, now, I'd watched enough *CSI* episodes to know that I was supposed to keep this guy talking. But with the way his story had just taken a sharp swerve into Creepsville, I wasn't so sure I wanted to!

Emmet was nodding his head now like an oversize bobblehead. "So guess what I did?" he asked me.

"What'd you do?" squeaked my support animal.

Thankfully, the guy was too into his story to notice. "I ran out into the hall, of course! I thought there must be a fire or something. But there *was* no fire."

Now his voice had taken on a creepy edge. The eyes in his pale, pimply face were practically pulsing with excitement.

"Then what?" squeaked a voice (me, this time). Yeah, I was starting to feel the goose bumps coming on strong.

"Then I saw there was nobody out there. No one at all! I was all alone. All the lights off, not another sound in the entire stage. And then came that awful, wailing *scream*."

All of a sudden, this horrible, spine-chilling, hair-raising, bloodcurdling shriek split the air! My heart nearly leaping out of my throat, I shouted, *"DUDE, WHAT WAS THAT?!"*

Emmet's lips curved down in an embarrassed frown. "Just a sound effect from my Nagra," he said sheepishly, clicking off the machine's power button. "It's from another movie I'm working on, a teen horror comedy."

"Bro, you scared the BREAKFAST BURRITO out of me!" I shouted.

"Sorry, but that's exactly how I felt, too!" he hissed. "Only the scream *I* heard was *ten times* as terrifying as that one!"

Whatever. "So, what happened next?"

"Not too much. I realized that it had to be a ghost! What else could scream like that? So I ran back into the room. Locked the door. Waited until one of the guards was making his rounds, then got the heck off the lot. Next day, I hear that Karin had vanished. And I knew it *had* to be the ghost! The tendrils. The scream. I know what I saw and heard!"

"Wait, but if you saw the creepy mist and heard that wailing scream, why are you sticking around on set? Aren't you scared the ghost could come for you next?"

"Yeah, a little scared, I guess. But the main reason I'm sticking around is because I'm gonna catch it!"

I frowned. "You mean, like, Ghostbusters-style, with a proton pack?"

"Nah, I mean on this! My Nagra III. I'm gonna prove that there really was a ghost in here and that everyone who claims they've seen it isn't making things up."

"Who else claims they've seen it?"

"Miguel Morales, for one. I think he was the first person to see the ghost. But I haven't even gotten a chance to talk to him about it, because no one's seen him in weeks." A look of worry scrunched his features. "I think the ghost probably got him."

"Anybody else see the ghost?"

"There's also Sophie, the night janitor. I think she might've actually been in here on the night of the most recent kidnapping, when Robert Villegas was taken. Robert was nice . . . Gonna miss him." Staring off across the stage, Emmet scratched his chin and frowned. "Yeah, so that's enough ghost stories for one morning. Let's get busy. They're filming an action sequence tomorrow and we'll have the stuntman on set."

"Is that Manny Martinez?"

"Yeah, yeah. He's a cool dude. Does all the risky stunts. Come to think of it, you look a lot like him."

Right then, this sort of proud but embarrassed blush began to crawl up my neck and face. It was such a weird feeling. I almost couldn't even look at Emmet as I said, "Nah . . . I mean, you really think so?"

"Oh yeah. Hey, you two related?"

"Related? Ha." *That's actually a good question, bud. Maybe you could tell me.* "I wouldn't bet on it," I said, trying to play off my nervousness.

"Yo, where should I put these?" A couple of beefy guys in FedEx uniforms were rolling in stacks of boxes on moving carts.

"Leave them there," Emmet told him. "That's fine. Thanks." Then he turned to me and said, "C'mon, those are the new stunt harnesses. Should've been here two days ago. We better get those unboxed and organized before Mr. Ultio, the director, comes out of his trailer and sees them, or you'll get to witness a 'Hurricane Harry' firsthand!"

CHAPTER 14

You wouldn't think so, but unloading about two dozen boxes full of heavy nylon harnesses is some seriously backbreaking work. I probably lost half my body weight in sweat and pulled at least three different muscles in my lower back. After we'd unloaded the harnesses, Emmet sent me to the storage room to drag out all the safety mats and stack them by the monkey bars, which turned out to be some kind of fly wire scaffolding for tomorrow's stunts. Then I had to find, dust, and drag out all the rolls of fly wire and stack them neatly up next to the mats.

The worst part was that the big guy could've done all this without even breaking a sweat. But he couldn't help me if anybody else was around, and there was *always* somebody around. I was exhausted, and it wasn't even noon! I had never been happier to hear somebody shout, "Lunch break!"

After a quick swing by the catering tables in the back, Liza, Ernie, Carter, and I found ourselves a nice little spot in a prop closet to eat our lunch and discuss what we'd been able to dig up so far. Through a mouthful of ham and cheese sandwich, I gave them the scoop about Emmet's encounter of the ghostly kind and the night janitor, Sophie, who claimed to have seen the thing, which of course had Liza and Ernie on the edge of their seats. Well, at least on the edge of the prop treasure chests we were all sitting on. We decided Sophie was our number one lead at the moment, and that our best bet would be to stick around today after hours to have a chat with her. Ernie, on the other hand, thought he'd already solved the case. He was convinced that the creepy clapper (the guy who holds the clapper board and yells "Action!") was the kidnapper.

"He just has that dead-eyed villain stare," Ernie told us. "You know, like the Borg Collective."

I didn't know. I was way out of the loop when it came to Star Trek baddies.

Liza hadn't started building her suspect list yet. She said they'd been pretty busy all morning, but she got all excited to tell us how she'd met the lead actor, Eduardo Cruz. It was weird to see the calm and calculated Liza all goo-goo-eyed and starstruck, talking about how handsome he was in real life and how nice he'd been when she happened to run into him by the actor trailers. The guy was a legit movie star, though, so who could blame her?

Carter didn't say much, just sat grumpily eating his grub (and *my* dessert Popsicle), and I knew it was because he was still upset over me not letting him play on the "monkey bars," so I said, "Look, if we have time and *nobody's* around, you can play on the monkey bars, all right?"

The chupacabra suddenly leapt to his big hairy feet. "¿De verdad, Jorge? You mean it?"

"Yes, yes, now take it easy. Remember, stay in character!"

"You pinkie and fang swear?" he said very seriously all of a sudden.

I sighed. "Yeah, I pinkie and fang swear. Happy now?"

"Very happy!" Carter showed us all his mouthful of gleaming fangs.

And suddenly—

The scream had come from that dusty old sarcophagus!

And naturally, the four of us responded in kind: "AAAAAHHHHHHHHH!"

The next thing we knew, the lid of King Tut's tomb flew open on its giant hinges and a pair of hands shot straight up, fingers clawing wildly at the air!

"It's King Tut!" cried Ernie as the four of us shrank back against the wall in wide-eyed terror. "He's come back for his *revenge*!"

I almost believed him, too!

"That's not actually his *real* tomb," Liza pointed out, "and this isn't a mummy movie, but I'm not going to lie—I'm still just as scared as you!"

"Let's get out of here before that thing comes out and curses us to our doom!" shouted Ernie.

But before we could move, out of the giant sarcophagus emerged not an embalmed and mummified corpse (which, by the way, we were all *extremely* thankful for), but . . . a spiffily dressed dude in a beige business suit.

"Whoa. I was expecting a lot worse," I admitted.

The man nodded understandingly. "My mother said the same thing when I was born."

"Well, if you're not a mummy, what are you?!" I shouted.

"The name's Lee. Albert Lee," he said coolly. "I'm a film agent."

"But what were you doing in King Tut's tomb?!" Liza wanted to know.

"Raiding it for treasure." He rolled his eyes at us. "Sleeping, of course!"

"Sleeping?"

"Sure! That is, until you four woke me up just

now. I always sneak in here to take naps when I'm in desperate need of inspiration. I grew up in the theater. My mother owned a playhouse. As a little boy, I fell in love with the smell of dusty old props. And do you want to hear a little secret? A good prop room nap hasn't failed me yet!" His intelligent brown eyes were locked on Carter, and he was grinning like a chupacabra at a goat convention. "Good morning, beautiful! What do they call you?"

The big guy was looking a little bit unsure. He glanced between Liza, Ernie, and me about a dozen times before putting out a feeler: "Carter?"

"Carter!" erupted Albert. "I. LOVE. THAT. NAME! I love everything about you!"

He scanned the chupacabra from head to toe and an inch at a time. "And what a costume! So realistic! So BOLD!"

Then came the cherry on top: he sniffed Carter's hairy armpit!

"You even smell like a real wild animal!" he cried ecstatically.

Liza double-face-palmed herself. Who could blame her?

"I bet you even made this costume yourself," Albert told Carter.

The chupacabra shrugged. "I was born like this."

"Of course you were! You're method to the bone, and I *dig* it!" Mr. Agent Man whirled around to face us, his expression suddenly serious. "You do realize that if *anybody* in this studio gets wind that you three are passing off a person in costume as a pet, not only will this furry genius here be arrested, but all of you would be summarily thrown off the lot, yes?"

"Oh no! Mister, please don't tell on us!" Ernie begged him.

"No worries, young man! I will do no such thing!" Albert assured us. "*Why*? Because I completely get what you're doing!"

I really didn't think that was possible, but what I said was "You do?"

"Yes, you're passing him off as your"—he leaned forward to read what it said on Carter's badge—"*emotional support animal* as part of his method acting training! It's genius, really! I wish more actors were as dedicated to their craft as this young man."

Liza, Ernie, Carter, and I all blinked slowly around at one another. It wasn't a bad excuse, actually. I said, "Uh, how'd you figure us out, sir?"

"Simple!" said the agent man. "Because I can *sense* talent! That's my SUPERPOWER! And I've never sensed this much natural acting prowess in my entire life!"

He was sensing something, all right. But it sure wasn't acting talent.

Albert swung around to gaze adoringly upon the big guy. "Your animal magnetism is simply undeniable!"

Well, at least he's right about that, I thought.

Then, snapping his eyes back to us again, he said, "I only make one request of you all, and his little secret stays between the five of us."

"What's the request?" Liza asked.

"Let me take him!"

"*What?* Take him where?!" I shouted.

"To Stage 5! There's a director there filming a picture about a family of yetis, and he's in desperate need of a leading man! Someone who can fully embrace the animal within!" He turned to Carter, his face practically glowing with excitement. "I'm going to make you the biggest box office draw since Iron Man! What do you say, friend?"

Carter appeared to think about it. "I always wanted to be in da movies..."

"There it is! Come with me, you beautiful creature!" Snatching Carter's hand, he began leading him toward the door of the prop room.

"Wait, no!" I shouted.

"Don't worry, he's safe with me!" Albert assured me. But it wasn't Carter's safety that I was worried about.

"When are you going to bring him back, though?" I said.

When? After I've made him a STAR!

CHAPTER 15

Albert promised us that Carter would meet us back at the studio around 6:00 p.m., when the place closed for the day.

We were fine with that because the plan was to stick around and have a talk with Sophie the night janitor, anyway.

My only hope was that the big guy didn't run into any goats between now and then, because if he did, things could get pretty dicey pretty *fast*.

Anyway, there were about a million more safety mats to drag out of the back and a zillion boxes to unpack, and by the time the set coordinator finally shouted, "Cut!" on the workday, I felt more exhausted than one of Santa's little helpers on Christmas Eve.

As I was getting ready to go, Second Assistant Director Lola went marching past my area with her clipboard for probably the tenth time that day, and like those ten other times, she smiled at me and waved and said something like, "What brave kids! What hardworking kids!"

Only little did she know that our *real* hard work had just begun.

It was time to question our first witness.

Sophie showed up just as almost everyone else was filing out through the enormous hangar doors. She came in pushing a cleaning cart stacked with brooms, buckets, and spray bottles, but if that wasn't enough of a giveaway, her dark blue coverall read: SOPHIE.

"There she is!" Ernie hissed excitedly from the captain's chair of the galaxy-consuming intergalactic spaceship where we'd been waiting. We all leapt to our feet.

"Let's make our move!" whispered Liza.

Sophie had made her way over to the catering area and was in the process of emptying a trash bin when we came up behind her.

"Hi," I said.

Yep, it was her, all right. She was as jumpy as someone who'd—well, seen *a ghost.*

"So sorry we startled you!" Liza told her, flicking some walnuts out of her hair.

I pinched my nose against the stink of rotting fish. "Yeah, so sorry . . ."

Sophie, with one hand over her probably pounding heart, smiled with relief and said, "Oh, no. It's not your fault! I get a little nervous whenever I work this particular stage."

Ernie gave her his most innocent look. "*Really?* Why?"

"*So* sorry about this mess," she said with an embarrassed frown, helping us pick the trash off ourselves. "But you three haven't heard?"

"Heard what?" Liza said, putting on a pretty convincing innocent look herself.

Now Sophie just looked confused as she picked a banana peel off my head. "Are you three new here?"

"Yeah, we're interns," Ernie answered. "Today was our first day."

"Well, *quit* today!" she shouted. "Leave this place and don't come back! It's HAUNTED!"

I shook my head. "Haunted?"

Sophie leaned in close as she whispered, "You haven't heard about the missing people?"

"We might have heard something," said Liza, playing it slick. "What about them?"

"They haven't walked out on the job like some people say. They've been kidnapped!"

"How can you be so sure?" Liza asked.

"Because two of them were my friends," said Sophie. "Constance Rodriguez and Miguel Morales. Miguel vanished over three weeks ago. Just disappeared right off set! The studio execs claimed he'd been planning on quitting because he didn't like how the movie was turning out, but that's not true! I never heard him say that even once! And Constance, they say, got spooked by the ghost, which is total hogwash! Constance was one of the people imploring the crew to remain calm, telling everyone that there was nothing mysterious happening on set. Then, out of the blue, *she* vanishes, too! They were both kidnapped, I tell you! And I know who did it, too! It was the ghost!"

"What makes you so sure there's a ghost in this stage?" Ernie asked with a pretty embarrassing tremble in his voice.

CHAPTER 16

"It happened just a few nights ago—not twenty yards from the *very* spot we're standing on!"

Sophie's voice had dropped to a creepy campfire-story whisper. "I was mopping the floors back by Mr. Ultio's trailer."

She pointed suddenly with her duster. "You know him, right? He's the director. He made that wonderful miniseries about the dancing Siamese cats. Have you seen it?"

We all shook our heads no.

"Anyway, I'd seen Robert Villegas, the screenwriter, go into Mr. Ultio's trailer. Mr. Ultio had already left for the day. I saw Robert go in and then come running out. Then, a few minutes later, I saw him go running in again. It seemed like something was wrong. Robert had his cell phone in one hand like he was trying to call someone, but the reception in this stage is terrible. Maybe ten minutes later, I hear a scream from inside the trailer. This blood-curdling cry of horror!"

Hmm. So she'd heard the same scream that Emmet had.

"Not a man's scream," Sophie went on. "Definitely not Robert's. But it had *most* definitely come from Mr. Ultio's trailer. Naturally, I ran over to see if someone was hurt. Injured, maybe. But there was no one in the office... not a soul! I wasn't sure what to make of it. I felt like I'd fallen into some dreadful nightmare. I made myself believe that the scream had come from outside the stage, from somewhere—anywhere—else, so I could finish cleaning the place.

"A few minutes later, I went back into Mr. Ultio's trailer to vacuum, as I do every evening—and that's when my vacuum started making these strange noises. Hideous shrieking and rattling sounds. At first, I thought something must have gotten stuck in the roller. And as I bent down to check, I sensed her—the ghost! It was La Llorona!"

"Whoa, whoa, whoa!" Ernie and I screeched in

unison. "How do you know it was La Llorona?"

"Because it makes perfect sense that it's her," Sophie said. "I bet she's haunting this stage because they're making a movie about her and she doesn't like it at all. I'm telling you, this stage has now become the real-life *Curse of La Llorona*!"

"Hold on a sec. Did you say you *sensed* or *saw* the ghost in question?" Liza asked.

Sophie looked annoyed. "Does it matter? Her presence was unmistakable!"

"But did you actually *see* it or not?"

"Well, not with my physical eyes, if that's what you mean. But I'm a little psychic. I come from a long line of fortune tellers. We are very attuned to the presence of ghosts and such."

"I bet," Liza said, giving her a look. "So then you didn't actually see a ghost."

"No, I did! But like I'm telling you—with the eyes of my mind!"

At this, Liza rolled the eyes of her head but didn't press further.

"Go on," Ernie said nervously.

Sophie's dark eyes focused. "Where was I? Oh, yes. So, from where I was kneeling in the room, I felt

She moved through the room as soundless as —well, a ghost!

her pass through the wall behind Mr. Ultio's desk—and then she was gone!

"I know you'll probably find this humorous," she said in an embarrassed way. "But I believe a bit of La Llorona's essence got sucked into the vacuum as she passed by me. I didn't *see* this happen, of course"—she shot Liza a quick glare—"but I know it happened!"

With her brows raised skeptically, Liza pointed at the shiny stand-up vacuum on her cleaning cart. "Is that the vacuum?"

"Oh, no, no!" gasped Sophie. "I wouldn't touch that thing again even for the role of Wonder Woman! I left it in the janitor's closet in the back. Haven't so much as looked at it since."

"Did you tell the police your theory?"

"I did. But they looked at me like my head hadn't been screwed on straight. I don't blame them, though. I didn't think a vacuum could be haunted, either, until I witnessed it firsthand. That's why I told the staff coordinator, 'You either find me a new vacuum or find yourself a new janitor!' I don't ever want to see that thing again. Listening to it shriek was probably the scariest experience of my life since the small part

I played in the horror movie *Ponies from Planet Evil*.

"They didn't tell any of us extras that the toy ponies could actually move *and* neigh!" she said. "It caught me completely by surprise! I thought those evil little things had actually come to life!" She paused, her eyes flicking to me. "By the way, did any of you see that movie?"

We all shook our heads. "I don't think so," I said.

"Oh, you should definitely give it a watch! Scariest toy movie of the early nineties. You'll see me at exactly forty-seven minutes and fifteen seconds. I'm one of the waitresses in the diner."

"I'll set a reminder on my TV," I lied.

"So you're an actress?" Ernie asked.

Sophie shrugged. "Ninety-nine percent of everyone who lives here is. The city workers, the salon owners. Even my gardener. I consider this job research, anyway. There's this role I'm trying to land. It's in a paranormal thriller with Frad Bitt!"

"What happened next?" Liza said. "After you sensed the ghost had vanished."

Sophie blinked, as if trying to rewind time with her mind. "Nothing. I ran out of the stage, so fast I'm surprised I didn't set off the fire alarm! The next morning, I find out that Robert's gone missing and that I was the last person to see him. The only reason I'm still working this stage is because if La Llorona nabs me, I'll get invaluable experience for the role I told you about. See, in the movie, the character I want to play gets kidnapped by a ghost. They'd practically have to give me the part, then!"

¡Órale! Actors . . . They're actually willing to get kidnapped by a ghost for a movie role! At least she's dedicated.

"What about these cameras?" Liza asked, pointing up at the sleek, silvery rectangle of the one above our heads. "Did they catch the ghost?"

Sophie was shaking her head. "Nope. The cameras are only here in the main area and in the halls by the offices," she explained. "Not inside the individual offices. They haven't caught anything. At least not that I've heard. And that's one of the biggest mysteries about the disappearances. No one suspicious is ever seen coming in or out of the stage. The victims are always here one second, then gone the next." She gave another small shrug. "It's no mystery to me, though, seeing as I know it's La Llorona behind it all. But it sure has the police baffled."

"Has anyone else seen or heard anything?"

"Oh, certainly!" said Sophie. "I'm pretty sure almost everyone on the crew has at one point or another. Well, everyone except for Max Spyder. He's the costume and special effects whiz kid on the set. You've probably heard of him. He's won over two dozen awards for his work on ghosts and ghost costumes, which is kind of ironic." Sophie paused, looking thoughtful. "No, I don't think he's ever been around anytime La Llorona's been spotted."

"Never?"

"Not once!" said Sophie. "How funny is that?"

Liza and I locked eyes. Funny? Not really. More like super suspicious!

And the cherry on top of this banana split of suspiciousness? His name *also* didn't appear on the to-be-kidnapped list.

Oh man. This case was getting more and more interesting by the second.

CHAPTER 17

After we'd all said bye to Sophie, Liza motioned for us to follow, and the three of us walked back across the stage, toward the back. There was a long hallway leading away from the main area, then a door that led to a few offices. When we reached it, Liza stationed Ernie and me there as lookouts.

"Wait here," she said. "If you see anyone coming, make a birdcall!"

"A birdcall?" Ernie whispered nervously. "I don't know any birdcalls!"

"Hey, where are you going?" I hissed at Liza.

"I saw the janitor's closet this morning while running an errand," she said. "I want to check out that 'haunted' vacuum cleaner Sophie mentioned. Be right back!"

What felt like a year later but was really only five

or six minutes, Liza came hustling back. To the untrained eye, it didn't look like she'd found anything, but that wide, Cheshire cat grin on her face told me otherwise. "What'dya got?" I whispered.

"Oh, just this!" said Liza.

Ernie's eyes bugged. "Oh, wow! That's a . . . uh, what is *that*?"

Liza was all smiles. "That's the ghost in the machine, you could say. Or in the vacuum, anyway. I found this in the air hose. I've helped my dad clean enough times to know what it sounds like when a vacuum bites off more than it can chew."

I caught her drift. "You mean, the horrible shrieks and rattling sound Sophie heard?"

"Exactly! So much for a haunted vac, huh?"

Ernie said, "Looks like a head that came off some action figure."

"That's what I was thinking," I admitted. Maybe King Midas's G.I. Joe or something, with that solid-gold look.

E-dog swung his concerned brown eyes questioningly up to Liza's. "What do you think this means?" he asked.

Pigtails Sherlock shrugged. "A little early to say, since I don't even know what it is yet. But Sophie was the last person in that room. Besides Robert and whoever kidnapped him, of course. And *this* was in the room at the exact time of the incident."

"Oh, and don't forget the ghost," Ernie pitched in. When Liza and I gave him a double dose of *You've-got-to-be-kidding* looks, he said, "What? It's not like we haven't run into a haunted piñata and a screaming sombrero! Is a crying lady ghost that much more unbelievable?"

I hated to admit it, but he had a point.

Ten minutes later, we were standing outside of Stage 21 in the fading flames of a Los Angeles sunset, waiting for Carter and his sarcophagus-napping superagent buddy to show.

The studio lot was as quiet, lonely, and deserted as it probably ever got. Which is to say, I only spotted two X-Men (Wolverine and Storm), Captain Jack Sparrow, Batman, Iron Man, a golf cart–driving Indiana Jones, and the Cowardly Lion from Oz.

"I don't see Carter anywhere," Ernie said with a worried frown.

I shrugged. "Hey, at least he'll blend in."

Suddenly, there came the huge throaty growl of about four hundred horses as a stretch limo roared up across the street from us.

"Man, I wonder which A-lister that belongs to," I murmured.

"Probably Tom Cruise," said Ernie. "Or maybe Robert Downey Jr."

Not bad guesses. But he wasn't even close.

"CARTER, WHERE'D YOU GET THIS THING?!" Liza shrieked as the three of us quickly piled into the plush, all-leather-everything interior. I mean, what planet were we on?

"Benito Delgado gave it to me," revealed the chupacabra, beaming at us.

"Are you talking about Mr. Delgado, the owner of Multiversal Studios?"

"Yep! Nice guy. Albert took me to see him. Oh, and dat's my new driver. Larry, these my amigos I was tellin' you 'bout!"

In the driver's seat, Larry, a very serious-looking hombre with beady eyes and thin, humorless lips beneath a thick handlebar moustache, nodded at us in a very serious way. Then he hit a button on the roof and up slid the glass privacy divider.

Carter learned over to whisper, "So did you catch the entrepreneur?"

"I think you mean 'saboteur,'" said Liza. "But no, not yet. We have a lead, though. A good one."

While we'd been standing out in front of the studio, waiting for Carter, Ernie had remembered overhearing some of the electrical department staff talking about a party up in the Hills tonight. A party being thrown by none other than Max Spyder himself, the special effects guy Sophie had mentioned.

At the time, it obviously hadn't meant much to Ernie. But now that Max had suddenly found himself on our short (and I mean *extremely* short) list of suspects, it was just the break we needed. A house full of guests (if we could sneak our way into the party, of course) would give us plenty of opportunity to go gumshoeing around his pad. Then we could figure out real quick if Mr. Spyder was up to any "paranormal" activities.

"If we're going to crash this party," said Liza, "we've got to fit in. We're going to need some cool clothes."

"Oh, dat's good, 'cause I bought you some!" said Carter excitedly. "When we went shopping for my suit!"

Ernie couldn't have looked any more excited if Captain Kirk himself was baking him a key lime cheesecake. "Seriously?"

"Uh-huh!"

"Where are they?"

Carter's grin somehow got even fangier. "I show you..."

Twenty minutes later, we were pulling up to an

all-glass high-rise building and Carter was leading us inside.

"Benito ask me where I was staying. I told him in da woods. And he said, 'No star of mine gonna live in da woods!' Then I tole him, 'Why not? Da woods is nice!' And he start cracking up and say he wanna put me in some comedy movies, too!" Carter beamed at us, a twinkle showing in those hungry bloodsucker eyes. "He already put me in one movie. Is a historical picture. I'm gonna be an army general."

Then he showed us the script with his name on it. "Carter, you can't accept this role!" I shouted.

The big guy frowned. "Why not?"

"Because you're not an actor in a suit! You *are* the suit! Those claws and teeth—that's really *you*!"

"And I'm beautiful, huh?" He was staring at his fangy mug in a fancy handheld mirror he'd found on the hallway table. ¡Órale! Just forty-eight hours in L.A. and he was already a diva!

"Carter, you just can't, okay? Imagine what would happen if someone finds out what you are. It's too risky!"

With a sigh, Carter took a little rectangle of paper out of his suit pocket and made like he was going to tear it in half. It looked like a receipt or something, so I said, "Hold up. What is that?"

"A check Mr. Delgado gave me for signing da movie contract." Carter looked sadly down at it. "But you right, Jorge. I jess gonna rip it up."

"Wait, let me see that," I said. I opened the check. My eyes nearly flew out of my face and took a lap around the room. I'd never seen so many zeroes *in my life*.

Ernie had been paging through the screenplay. Now he peeked over my shoulder at the check. "THAT MUCH MONEY FOR A NONSPEAKING ROLE?!"

Carter nodded. "Uh-huh."

"You don't have to talk or anything? Just growl and look scary?"

Carter nodded again. "Uh-huh."

"Dude, you GOTTA do it!" I shouted, gripping the bloodsucker by the shoulders. "This is the opportunity of a lifetime! You can't pass this up!"

I'd never seen a chupacabra look so confused. "But I thought you jess said it was too risky, Jorge."

"Yeah, I know what I said," I told him. "But I just thought of about a hundred thousand reasons to change my mind!"

CHAPTER 18

Carter wasn't kidding when he said he'd bought us some new threads. As a matter of fact, he'd bought us an entire closet's worth of new threads. And the closet just so happened to be the size of a small *department store*. It was like walking into a forest of fancy suits, rhinestone-studded dresses, and faux furs so thick and real looking that you could've confused Liza, Ernie, and me for Carter's kid siblings.

The party was up in the Bird Streets—the supercool neighborhood in the Hollywood Hills above Sunset Strip that looks out over the iconic skyline of Los Angeles. Liza had found Max Spyder's address online by hacking a local pizza shop's client directory, and when the clock struck eight, we had Larry, Carter's personal chauffeur, limo us over.

The drive itself was pretty awesome. This was only

my second ride ever in a limousine, and I know that for most kids it might not be such a huge deal, but I grew up hardly being able to afford a seat on the public *bus*.

Even with a ton of traffic, the ride over to Max's felt short, mostly because there were a zillion things to do in the limo, which, by the way, came with its own flat-screen TV *and* PlayStation! When we got there, we knew we'd found the right place because the street looked like the parking lot for a Taylor Swift concert, with cars lining both sides of the narrow street and even spilling out of driveways.

We followed the pulse and throb of party music about a block and a half up the hill and—*boom!*—there it was, Max's house.

"Nice party," Ernie said.

"Very nice," agreed Liza.

"I gotta pee," said Carter.

I turned to the sports coat–wearing Dracula. "Can it wait until we get inside? I'm sure Max has a bathroom."

The chupacabra shook his furry head. "But I don't wanna use a people bathroom."

"Why not?"

"'Cause Albert told me it was important for my acting training to *stay in character*. I'm gonna be playing a wild animal, remember?"

"Stay in character? Carter, you *are* the character!"

Still, we found the big guy a nice clump of trees between the houses, and while Carter did his business, our fancy shoes carried us up the gravelly slope toward Max's house.

We'd barely made it halfway up the driveway to the large stone fountain with its family of stony flamingos arcing water out of their beaks when we got cut off by this buff bodybuilder type with muscles so big you felt bad for his T-shirt.

"Can I help you?" he asked.

"Oh, hi!" Liza said with a friendly wave. "We're here for the party."

"Is your name on the list?" asked Muscles.

"No, but we're working on a movie with—"

"You can't come in," interrupted Muscles.

"But we know Max," I told him. "We work together."

His eyes flicked down to his clipboard. "Are your names on the list?"

Ernie said, "No, but that's probably because somebody forgot to—"

"You can't come in." They seemed like his favorite four words.

¡Fantástico! I thought. We'd run into the human party pooper! There was no way around this guy and unfortunately there was absolutely no way *through* him. He could probably bench-press our combined weight as easily as I could lift a pencil.

Just as we turned away

from the house, with Liza probably already trying to figure out another way in, I saw the moonlit form of our tuxedo-rocking chupacabra coming up the slope of the driveway toward us.

And from back toward the house, I heard, "Yo, Carter! What's up, you animal?"

"¡Hola, Jake!" The big guy strolled right past us and up to Muscles.

"Gimme some fur, buddy!" said the clipboard-wielding brick wall.

"Uh, you two know each other?" I asked, trying not to sound as shocked as I felt.

"We met at the audition for my new movie!" said Carter.

"This guy's amazing!" said Muscles, slinging a beefy arm around Carter. "I've never seen anyone sink their teeth into a character like him!"

He was probably right about that, too.

"Estos son mis amigos," he told Muscles—er, Jake—and suddenly the human roadblock looked a touch embarrassed.

"Aww, I had no idea you three were with Carter! You should've said something!" he told us.

"I really shouldn't do this," whispered Jake with a mischievous grin, "but since Carter's name's already on the list, I'm just gonna write you all in." He grinned over at the big guy. "Anything for a pal!"

CHAPTER 19

Walking in through the front door of Max's house, I saw so many famous stars, I thought we'd floated up into outer space! The party was already in full swing, and there was hardly any room to move anywhere in the ginormous living room, or even out in the pool area beyond the wall of sliding glass doors. Everybody was here—and I mean *everybody*.

The plan was simple. Step one: *mingle*. That part was easy. We just floated around, patting total strangers on the arms and backs, fake-laughing our heads off every time anyone said anything even remotely funny, and ignoring the weird *Who-the-heck-are-those-kids?* looks everybody was giving us as we worked our way through the room.

Step two: *find Max's secret studio*. Surprisingly, that part wasn't too hard, either.

"It's actually not so secret," said this random dude we'd been pumping for info (who turned out to be Max's hairstylist). "I think his studio is just down in the basement."

Surprise número dos: no heavy-duty security system. In fact, there wasn't even a door. We basically just waltzed into it. Though we did have ourselves a little scare in the process... We were down the stairs and a couple of steps into the nearly pitch-black

Wayne Bronson, star of about a dozen action blockbusters

Ebenezer Dylan, world famous dog-whisperer

Richard Prinze, top-three funniest stand-up comics of all time room when I saw a ghostly clawed hand reach out of the darkness for Ernie!

"DUDE, WATCH OUT!" I cried, yanking him just out of reach. "IT'S LA LLORONA!"

Liza smashed the light switch on the wall. Two rows of bright overhead strip lights buzzed instantly to life.

As it turned out, the hand belonged to a costumed mannequin, not the vengeful undead weepy lady.

Emmet, our much less famous coworker, but a cool dude nonetheless

Tayra, world-famous pop superstar

Eduardo Cruz, epic movie star and the lead in The Curse of La Llorona

Ernie gave a *Mommy-I'm-scared*-level gulp. "Something tells me we found our bad guy."

"Beautiful, aren't they?" said a voice.

I'm not going to lie. When you're sneaking around somebody's house, trying not to get caught, and suddenly you hear an unfamiliar voice right behind you in the dark, it can be pretty terrifying. Did I pee my pants? That's a negative. But it had been a *close* call...

Cuatro cabezas and four pairs of eyes snapped instantly around. It was Max! Max Spyder, the costume designer and special effects whiz kid! I recognized him from the studio directory by the clock-in machine in Stage 21.

"Scratch that," Ernie hissed into my ear. "Looks like the bad guy found *us*!"

"Stay cool," I hissed back.

Between us, Max lifted his champagne glass toward the brightly lit display of ghost costumes and said, "Those are my pride and joy."

"Dey very interesting," said the big guy with a nervous, fangy grin.

"And so are you." Max's bright blue eyes had locked onto Carter. "Where in the world did you find fangs like that? Make those yourself?"

"You could say he was born with them," I told Max.

He grinned.

Nice! Are they acrylic or porcelain?

"Maybe da second one," mumbled Carter.

"Every single tooth looks incredible! I'd love to talk shop with you sometime." Max sounded more than a little impressed with the look of Carter's fangs. I bet he would've been even *more* impressed with their bite.

"So you collect ghost costumes?" Liza asked him, trying to sound all casual about it.

Max was grinning up at the display. "Yep! These are all replicas or the actual costumes we used on the last five movies I worked on."

"Really?"

"That's right. I've got them all here because for the past year or so, I've been working on a behind-the-scenes documentary on the costume-and-effects side of the biz. Sort of chronicling my life's work, mixing in old footage with stuff I'm doing now. I'm currently editing it." He raised his chin toward the wall of electronics in the corner, a massive PC with about three even more massive flat-screen displays that had the gamer in me itching to take them for a test drive. "It's fascinating stuff. Well, fascinating to me, anyway." He looked curiously between us. "You all are working on *The Curse of La Llorona*, right?"

"Yeah, yeah, we're the new interns!" said Ernie, his voice only shaking a little.

Max grinned at him. "Cool. Unfortunately, the ghost we're using in that movie is pure CGI—computer-generated imagery—so there's no real-life costume I can show you. But anyway, I'm glad you could make it to my party tonight."

"Yeah, thanks for inviting us!" I said, and Liza gave me a look like, *You seriously went there?*

Max, meanwhile, was frowning like maybe he wasn't so sure he *had* invited us. But what he said was "Don't mention it."

Suddenly, a face appeared at the top of the stairwell. "Max! Keith and Mariana are looking for you," they said. "Something about the water in your Jacuzzi turning purple or something."

Max sighed. He didn't look so happy at this news. "This is why you should *never* throw a pool party," he said to us. "See you upstairs."

The instant our gracious host had vanished up the steps, Liza rushed over to his computer and dropped into his ultra-cool gaming chair. Then, slipping a small USB stick out of her pocket, she plugged it into one of the ports on the side of the computer.

"Liza, what are you doing?!" Ernie whispered.

"What does it look like?" she said.

The three of us rushed over, crowding around her and peering over her shoulders. Liza's fingers danced across the keyboard, and a split second later, the login screen blinked out, and she was in! There was Max's desktop, with about a bazillion little icons. You could hardly even see his background, which was a picture of him with a famous director.

As Liza opened the computer's search function, I hissed, "What are you looking for?"

"Max's documentary," she said.

"Liza, we don't have time to watch that documentary, no matter how interesting it sounds!"

She turned her head to smack me with an eye roll. "This isn't for entertainment, Jorge. Max just gave me a great idea to prove—or maybe even disprove—our suspicions."

"How?" the big guy wanted to know, even as Liza's free hand slipped smoothly into her pocket and retrieved a small square of lined paper, which she unfolded and trapped under the edge of Max's keyboard. On the paper was what looked like a list of names, dates, and times.

"What is that?" I whispered, shooting a fast look over my shoulder to make sure nobody was watching us. The coast looked pretty clear. But how long would it stay that way?

I could feel my racing heart going *th-thump, th-thump, th-thump!* against my ribs. It wasn't a wonderful feeling.

"This is a list of all the kidnapped crew members with the dates and times of their kidnappings," Liza explained, clicking up a storm. "I wrote them all out, trying to see if I could find any connection between them, any sort of pattern. There didn't seem to be any. But..."

"But what?" hissed Ernie.

"Lookie here," said Liza, opening a file linked to a video-editing program. She'd found Max's documentary.

Suddenly, a door slammed somewhere, and the four of us nearly jumped out of our skins as a chorus of loud cheers ripped the tense silence in Max's studio!

"Liza, hurry!" whispered Ernie. "I don't know how much more suspense I can take!"

"But what's his documentary supposed to prove?" I asked Liza.

"Everything."

"Elaborate, please."

Only, Liza didn't. Instead she used the video's edit timeline to scroll through the documentary footage. "Liza, *hurry!*" Ernie hissed.

"Found it!" Now she slid the cursor over and clicked the big play button.

"Found what?" I whisper-shouted.

The video started to play, and the four of us watched as Max, swinging a teaching pointer, talked all excitedly about a big blanket-looking costume while also splicing in clips from the movie it had been featured in. The computer audio had been muted, but it looked like Max was showing off the costume's stitching. At first, I had no clue why Liza was wasting our time with this. But then she began circling the time stamp on the bottom left-hand corner of the video with the cursor, and my breath caught hot in my throat.

This footage had been recorded on the *same* day and at the *same* time as the first kidnapping!

Which meant...

"He wasn't there," I said in a half-stunned voice. Yep, Liza's genius had once again just smacked me across the face like a churro. A big sugary one. "I mean, he wasn't at the studio when the first kidnapping happened! He was right *here*."

"Now let's see if he was *also* here during kidnapping number two." Liza fast-forwarded the video, and next thing, we were watching Max and a couple buddies standing in front of a huge green screen, wearing those spandex onesies covered with motion sensors.

As Max slipped into another one of his ghost costumes, Carter breathed, "He wasn't there for that one, either."

Liza fast-forwarded the video again, and less than a minute later, it became pretty obvious that Max hadn't been anywhere near Stage 21 during *any* of the kidnappings. He'd been right here, working on his documentary.

Liza turned to look at us. Her face was a mixture of relief and disappointment. She said, "Looks like we need a new suspect."

We were back to square one.

CHAPTER 20

So the good news was that we hadn't been sneaking around in the basement of some sabotaging, ghost-impersonating kidnapper.

The bad news?

We'd just lost our only solid suspect.

The party was still in full swing by the time the four of us made it back upstairs, but since we all had an early start tomorrow, we decided to call it a night. But we'd only got as far as Max's foyer when all our plans of going home to a nice cozy bed and a flock of jumping sheep to count went right out the window.

Because the moment we turned the corner past the vintage jukebox, the four of us froze dead in our tracks.

This was what we saw:

At first, though, I wasn't even sure *why* we'd all stopped. My conscious mind hadn't quite caught up to what my *sub*conscious mind had already figured out.

Then my eyes zoomed in on the golden trophy in the moustache guy's hairy fist, and my eyes nearly hit the eject button in my face! The dude was holding an Oscar trophy.

But not just any Oscar trophy.

It was an Oscar trophy without *a head*...

Slowly, feeling the world seesaw around me, I turned to look at Liza, who, by the way, already had that little golden head out of her pocket and in the palm of her slightly shaking hand.

But Liza was nodding her head. "I kind of do."

"Are you two saying that *that guy* is the kidnapper?" Ernie hissed.

Pigtails Sherlock hadn't taken her brilliant eyes off the guy. "Impossible to say for sure."

I said, "Then again, if the shoes fits..."

"We need more info," Liza said. "C'mon!"

The guy was clearly telling some kind of story. You could tell by the way he was changing his voice and swinging his arms all over the place. It probably had to do with the trophy.

"If only Eduardo was still here!" he was saying as we approached. "He left just before we got here, but I so wanted to show him this! I think he'd have a good laugh! And he did totally deserve it for *The Desert Rose*."

Just as he said that, I came up beside Emmet and saw him crush the empty plastic cup he'd been sipping from. To me, it looked like an involuntary reaction. Like something someone had said had physically hurt him. "You all right?" I asked him

"Oh, hey, Jorge! Yeah, I'm fine, buddy. Cool that you could make it!"

"We were in the neighborhood," I said, trying to play it all cool. "Thought we'd swing by."

Liza, meanwhile, had caught the eye of the actor dude with the trophy. "Excuse me," she said, "is that Oscar yours?"

The actor, who I was pretty sure I recognized from some TV show, said, "If you mean, did I win this? Then *no*. But if you're asking whether I am now its new owner, then a resounding yes!" He grinned proudly down at the golden, headless man. "I just won it at the auction!"

The guy standing next to him, another actor maybe, sighed, looking annoyed. "Oh, quit rubbing it in, will you?"

Actor Número Uno's megawatt smile widened, nearly blinding me as he turned it on us. "I beat this sore loser right here by a measly buck! But the truth is, he never stood a chance!"

Actor Número Dos rolled his eyes. "It was a single-bid, secret auction," he told us. "If it had been open bid, I would've made absolutely *sure* I beat you."

The tall lady in the fancy black dress who I definitely recognized from TV (she was the head chef from a restaurant drama my abuelos never missed) said to us, "You should have seen them just now at the auction house. Like two toddlers fighting over a toy."

"A toy? Susan! How could you?" Still beaming, Actor Número Uno lifted the headless trophy over his own perfectly styled head of hair. "This is a genuine piece of Hollywood history!"

"Let them hold it, Keith," the lady told him. "Can't you see how they're looking at it?"

"Oh, sure. Here." Actor Número Uno passed the trophy to Liza.

With her own megawatt smile, Liza took it. "Thanks."

"How do you four know Max?" the actor lady asked us.

"We just got hired on Mr. Gomez's latest movie," I said. *"The Curse of La Llorona."*

And just as I said that, some friends of Actor Número Uno, Número Dos, Emmet, and the chef lady came over, distracting them. Liza immediately did what I was hoping she'd do.

She tried Cinderella's slipper on.

And it was a perfect fit!

Translation: the little golden head had come from that little golden body!

"*Bingo!*" Ernie whispered, then played it all cool, sort of whistling to himself and looking distractedly around as Liza slipped the golden head back into her pocket.

"Come on, Keith," said one of the new peeps to Actor Número Uno. "We have to hurry if we're going to make it."

He glanced down at his enormous fancy watch. "He's right, Suze. Let's run."

"Don't forget this!" Liza handed him the trophy back.

"Ah yes. Can't forget Oscar!" he said with a grin.

"I was wondering," said Liza as they all turned to go, "who owned it before you?"

"That'd be Mauricio Veralo. The renowned composer," said Actor Número Uno.

"Mauricio had it for years," said the famous lady. "It does have a fascinating story. It's messy, but quite compelling. I'd tell it to you, but you're better off hearing it from the horse's mouth, so to speak. A firsthand account is hard to beat. Ask

Mr. Gomez about it when you see him. He'll tell you the whole thing. And he tells it better than anybody!"

Suddenly, a terrifying, earsplitting shriek cut through all the music and party chatter. Everybody with a pulse gasped and jumped and whirled toward the sound, looking for the source of the blood-curdling cry.

"*IT'S LA LLORONA!*" somebody shouted.

"What was that?" Ernie's voice was a petrified squeak.

Then I saw what it was. Emmet and his silly audio recorder!

The guy just couldn't seem to help himself.

CHAPTER 21

The following day, as I made my way back toward the stunt department area of Stage 21, I kept my fingers crossed that Emmet had run out of boxes for us to unpack.

I had a sneaking suspicion that I'd been knighted the unofficial "unpacker" of the place, but wasn't sure my back muscles could take a second round. I was looking for Emmet when I spotted somebody else.

My entire body instantly froze up.

It was Manny. Manny Martinez.

It's hard to explain what I felt the first time I saw my maybe-dad, other than the whole "maybe" part dropping away the second I laid eyes on the dude.

Some things you just know. This was one of those things.

That was my dad.

And he looked more or less how I'd always pictured him, too.

Except... he wasn't a dad to me in any way that really mattered. I'm sure you've heard of stay-at-home dads, right?

Well, he was the opposite. He was a stay-*away* dad.

Those were the worst kind.

Next thing I knew, he'd caught me staring, and he smiled at me and raised his hand in a little wave. "Hey, Jorge!" he called over the shouts and stage sounds, and hearing him say my name for the first time was like winning a blue ribbon at the school talent show—*and* like getting kicked in the stomach by an angry mule. I'd never felt so mixed up inside about anything. Not ever. I couldn't even feel my lips move when I answered him back.

"Hi . . . *Dad*."

A look of confusion flitted across Manny's face. Slowly, he put down a couple of the metal bars. "Did you just call me—*Dad*?"

Realizing that I *had* just called him Dad and had almost totally blown my cover broke the spell. *"What?* No! I called you Chad."

His frown deepened. "But my name is Manny."

"I know that! I call all handsome Latino men Chad."

"Oh." He shrugged like, *Whatever.* "Anyway, you *are* Jorge, right? My new assistant?"

"Yeah, that's me."

"All right, well, let's get to work, 'cause we've got plenty of it!"

Judging from the mess of bolts, screws, and wrenches scattered all over the top of the stack of safety mats, it looked like we were going to be rebuilding Carter's monkey bars in a new spot. Manny started explaining how it was done, but it was hard to pay attention, because (a) I wasn't exactly the build-it-yourself type, and (b) I just couldn't concentrate!

Truth was, all my life, I'd wondered what this moment would be like—the moment when I'd finally see my dad face-to-face. And here was that moment. It was happening in the back of a movie set in L.A. Yeah, "weird" didn't begin to describe it.

"Hey, pay attention," Manny said when he caught me staring at him and not at the crossbar section that he was trying to show me how to attach. "I'm going to be jumping off this thing pretty soon. You've got to listen to me and do this *exactly* how I tell you."

"Why should I?" I snapped. "You're not my father!"

Yep. I said that. I hadn't even planned to say it, the words just spilled right out. I guess twelve years of pent-up anger and bitterness was an even more explosive combo than Coca-Cola and Mentos.

"Now, once we start building this thing," he said, "we'll have to work fast. Can't leave a bunch of small pieces lying around overnight to get lost. Is there anything you want to ask me before we start?"

"Yeah, why'd you leave us, huh?!" Oops again. I know it probably doesn't seem like it, but I *was* trying real hard to keep my emotions down. Honest.

Only they seemed to keep coming back up faster than my grandma's harder-than-rocks chicken enchiladas. It was obviously going to be a long day.

Manny shook his head at me. "What?"

"I—I meant yesterday. We had a ton of boxes to unpack! Where were you?"

He blinked. "It was my day off."

"Makes sense."

Picking up an Allen wrench, he said, "I gather you had a tough day yesterday?"

Yesterday? *Ha!* "Try the last *twelve years*, bud."

Manny turned to look at me again. "Wow. You're a little young to be so jaded, no?"

"No thanks to you," I mumbled.

"Huh?"

"Forget it."

Working alongside my dad in a movie studio was a totally surreal experience. I felt like I'd gotten stuck in some weird daydream, and I didn't know whether to feel happy or sad, depressed or completely over the moon.

The thing I felt for sure, though, was surprise. Manny really didn't seem like such a terrible guy. At least not as bad as I'd sometimes imagined him. He was quiet and hardworking and always looking out to make sure some heavy section of scaffolding wasn't about to split my head like a pea. Those were some pretty good dad qualities, even though he'd never been anything like a dad to me.

Our case, meanwhile—aka the entire reason we'd come to L.A.—had totally slipped my mind. I forgot to ask him anything about the kidnappings. Or the ghost. Or if he'd ever heard any juicy rumors about either on set. What a gumshoe I'd turned out to be, huh?

Anyway, Manny and I had managed to add almost a whole fifteen feet to the scaffolding when Liza and Ernie showed up for lunch. And they had some news.

Apparently, Liza had asked around and discovered that Archie Gomez, the producer whose production company we were trying to keep from going bankrupt, always had lunch at a certain table at a certain café in L.A. She thought maybe we could hustle over and ask Mr. Gomez if he could tell us the story about that decapitated Oscar. It was a pretty good plan. Especially since that little golden head was our best—and *only*—lead at the moment.

The café wasn't too far, less than a twenty-minute walk from the studio. As it turned out, though, there was no need to hoof it. The big guy had just come off the set of his movie and we all took the "Cartermobile" over.

On the way, we racked our noggins, trying to come up with a way to break the ice with Archie. It wasn't like we could just sit down at his table and start asking him a million and one questions—we had to be smooth about this. Problem was, no one could come up with any smooth way to do it. Fortunately, we wouldn't have to. Because as we came up to the little bayberry-hedged walk of the café, Mr. Gomez broke the ice for us!

CHAPTER 22

After the standard introductions (which didn't feel so standard when it was a chupacabra doing the introducing), we all sat down at Mr. Gomez's table and ordered lunch.

He told us to order whatever we wanted, even things that weren't on the menu, because he was good friends with the chef, so we did. Ernie and I had a hankering for meatball calzones, Carter went for a plate of blood sausage (no surprise), and Liza asked for a vegan omelet and chopped salad. Mr. Gomez, liking our calzone idea, ordered one for himself.

Archie turned out to be a super-nice guy. It made me feel even better about our decision to come help him and his company. He asked Carter how filming was going, and Carter said that it was great and asked him if he'd ever consider producing a new *Wizard of*

Oz movie, but with goats. Carter offered to play the lead role, and Mr. Gomez said that he would think about it.

Before we knew it, our food arrived, hot and steamy, and once we all had our napkins tucked into the front of our shirts, it was time for the real main course.

Liza said, super nonchalantly, "Mr. Gomez, you think you could tell us the story of the decapitated Oscar?"

It must've been some story—I saw his entire body stiffen in his seat. If I didn't know better, I would've thought the guy was choking on a meatball!

As a matter of fact, I did know better and I was *still* warming up the old Heimlich maneuver just in case, when he said, "Oh my. Are you sure you want to hear that story? It's quite involved."

So Liza told him about the actor who'd won the cabeza-less Oscar at the auction and that famous lady who'd told us to ask him about the story.

"Well, if you're interested," said Mr. Gomez, "I'll tell it. But the first thing you should know is that it really isn't a story about an award trophy. It's about the greatest actor I have ever met, Phineas Alcaraz."

"Oh, I've heard of him!" Ernie shouted. "He made

a guest appearance on *Star Trek* once! He did an awesome job, too."

"I'm not surprised," said Mr. Gomez. "Phineas could act anything—film, stage, TV. It didn't matter. A truly once-in-a-generation talent. He had a gift for being able to transform himself into any character he played. Any! It was a marvel to witness, like seeing magic in real life. Unfortunately, his genius was only matched by his ego and his notoriously foul temper. Everything on set, everything around him, had to be *precisely* how he envisioned it! Not a hair out of place, or he'd berate the hair and makeup team. Not a prop out of position, or he'd tear into the prop department. Before you knew it, he'd take over an entire production, overruling everyone and taking everyone's job, from the lighting staff to the director himself. And soon he'd plunge so deep into character that he would throw the script out the window, so to speak! He'd begin to create his own lines, his own dialogue, and he'd demand that everyone else develop lines that made sense with his—or find themselves another job. His ability to ad-lib was nearly unmatched throughout cinematic history, but not all actors excel in that, and few directors that I've ever worked with appreciate it very much. His reputation for being extremely difficult on set was one of Hollywood's most widely known secrets. His colleagues would nearly always, at some point in the shoot, stage a mutiny against Phineas. Of course, the worst and most notorious of these on-set battles occurred on a project I was producing, *The Desert Rose*."

"Dat's one of my favorites!" said Carter excitedly, and all I could do was give him an *Are-you-kidding-me?* look. I was pretty sure that movie was a medieval love story, and it didn't even show a single goat. Not even an actor in a goat costume.

"Your taste is impeccable, my friend," Mr. Gomez told the big guy. "You know, for some reason you remind me of an old and dear friend of mine named Carlos. Perhaps it's the fangs." Then, taking a deep breath, he said, "At any rate, everyone on set came together to confront Phineas over his tyrannical behavior—from Jane Robby, our cinematographer, to Miguel Morales, our production designer. But naturally he refused to give an inch. In fact, he became outraged that they would even have the gall to challenge him in such a brazen way! Then it became my problem. Phineas made me choose: I could either keep him on the movie, or the rest of the cast and crew—a team who, you should know, were all very dear friends and colleagues, people I genuinely loved working with and will always work with. I, of course, had to let my star actor walk. The following morning, Phineas Alcaraz was fired from the movie, and he was in such a rage that our stuntman, Manny

Martinez, had to physically restrain him and drag him off set while he hurled insults and objects at everyone. He gave Manny a black eye. I believe Manny gave him two in return.

"That week I found a suitable—though not quite as talented—replacement. Phineas vanished after I released him. For over a year, not a peep was heard from the man. No, not even a single photograph of him snapped! It was rumored that he'd left L.A. Maybe even California. In the coming months, *The Desert Rose*—which unsurprisingly wrapped quickly after Phineas's departure—went on to achieve critical acclaim, and was nominated for the granddaddy of all showbiz awards, an Oscar. And would you know it, on the very night of the ceremony, Phineas reappeared!"

"You got to be making this up," I said, dipping my calzone in some marinara sauce and taking a delicious bite.

"I wish I was," said Mr. Gomez sadly. "But I'm not. Phineas had slipped into the ceremony in disguise, impersonating another actor who had been invited but couldn't make it due to some unforeseen travel complications. Then, victory for the cast! We won! The Oscar for best actor went to Eduardo Cruz, our new leading man. And right as he went up onstage to accept his award, Phineas revealed himself! Snatching the Oscar from Eduardo's hand, he began making his own acceptance speech. He managed to insult every single cast and crew member, yours truly included, and claimed that he was the driving force behind what little the movie was actually able to achieve on-screen. He then proceeded to *smash* the award against the podium, and he decapitated the Oscar! He claimed the head as his prize for the injustice he'd suffered, and before security could apprehend him, Phineas pulled his second vanishing act."

For a moment Mr. Gomez sat staring quietly into his tall glass of lemon tea, his eyes dark and far away like they were scanning the pages of an old yearbook. "The Oscars committee, of course, replaced Eduardo's trophy, and the Oscar Phineas had decapitated was sold to movie memorabilia collectors. And now the whole sad tale has passed into Hollywood lore."

No one said anything for what felt like a very long time. Even a couple of the waiters who had been eavesdropping got back to work.

Finally, Liza asked, "What happened after? To Phineas, I mean."

Mr. Gomez gave a tired sigh, as if reliving the memory had exhausted him. "I don't think a single soul has seen him since. His first disappearance was impressive, but his second seems permanent. It has been over six years since anyone has seen him. Though, naturally, I have heard rumors."

"Like what?" asked Carter. The big guy's entire mouth was now completely splattered with marinara sauce. He'd taken my bowl (and Ernie's) and had been slurping the stuff like it was Pepsi. He looked like the world's filthiest raccoon. A raccoon trying to dress like George Washington. It was pretty much all I could do not to burst out laughing.

"I once heard from a friend who works for an airline," said Mr. Gomez, "that Phineas had left the country. But that is just he said, she said. No one knows whatever became of Phineas Alcaraz. And I doubt anyone ever will." His expression turned thoughtful. "It's interesting, but that dastardly night marked the height of my production company. Almost every subsequent movie has been a terrible flop. You can blame it on casting issues, budgetary oversights. Or simply the strange and unexplained, like now on *The Curse of La Llorona*. Of course, the tragedy of Phineas Alcaraz makes my company's financial plight seem like a trivial matter, indeed. I feel for Phineas, I truly do—wherever he might be."

"That's a heavy story," Ernie said, looking confusedly around for his bowl of marinara.

Archie sighed. "Phineas was a heavy individual. A genius, undoubtedly. A true virtuoso of the arts. But not a man to trifle with. No, not a man to trifle with at all..."

Mr. Gomez looked like he might've said more, but story time was over.

The paparazzi had found Carter!

CHAPTER 23

We now had a new suspect. And boy oh boy, was he a suspicious one! Talk about having a motive. Here was a guy with a notoriously awful temper and all the reasons in the world to want to tank Mr. Gomez's movie and, with financial domino effect, his entire production company.

"It has to be him!" Liza said on the ride back to the studio. She was on her phone, scrolling through the credits section of Mr. Gomez's award-winning movie, *The Desert Rose*. "Every single one of them, all the kidnapped crew, worked on *The Desert Rose*! Phineas is snatching all the people who worked on the movie they kicked him out of!"

I'm not going to lie—it seemed like a slam dunk. Plus, it wouldn't even be too hard to figure out if Phineas really was behind the kidnappings.

All we'd have to do was sneak into his house, snoop around a bit. Or better yet, we could have Pepe and some of his blood-slurping buddies keep a 24-7 watch on the guy, see where he went and if he did anything suspicious. It'd be easy.

Problem was, how do you track down a guy who's basically gone missing? That was the tricky part. Liza suggested we could try to look into some of the old studio's records, see if we could find an address. But that was going to take time, because she wasn't even sure where they kept those kinds of records. There was also another problem.

Phineas probably didn't even live at his old address anymore. Chances were he'd moved. I mean, I know I sure would have if I was trying to vanish off everybody's radar.

So how we were supposed to track down a living ghost? A dude who could jump into a costume and become pretty much anyone? The answer hit me just as the four of us were piling into the limo again after work. Question: Who knows where everybody lives?

The answer? The Department of Motor Vehicles, of course! Where driver's licenses are made—with people's addresses on them!

"You're brilliant, Jorge!" Liza screeched when I told her my idea. "They'll have records of pretty much everybody in the entire state!"

All we had to do now was figure out a way into the DMV. Walking in there with our brightest smiles and asking to paw through their files was a definite no go. This would require some serious sneaks.

Good thing for us that we knew just about the sneakiest critters on two legs: chupacabras!

After having Larry limo us over to Pepe's place, we met up with the bloodsucker and told him our plan. Pepe had a great idea about how we could sneak into the DMV (and a handy box of crayons—don't ask), and he drew it out for us.

You'd think tunneling under a strip mall would be pretty much impossible, what with the concrete and all. But I guess nothing was impossible when you were seven feet tall and had claws sharper than a polar bear's.

We let our computer whiz get right to work, and it only took Liza about two minutes to crack the system's password. "The system also links to the Department of State, so we'll be able to find anything and everything on this guy right here," she said, typing up a storm.

Meanwhile, Ernie and I tried to keep the two chupacabras from totally blowing the whole mission.

"Would you two PLEASE stop messing with the lights?" I snapped at Carter and Pepe. The two of them kept turning the mini spotlights above Liza's computer on and off and on and off and on and off again. "You guys are going to get us caught!"

"But it's so fun!" Pepe hissed with delight. "Watch! Daytime! Nighttime! Daytime! Nighttime again."

"Dude, STOP it!"

Thankfully, less than ten minutes later, Liza had found our man.

Bingo! The whole plan was working out perfectly!

That is, until Liza scrolled down and we saw the bad news.

Phineas's passport. The last time it had been used was over *five years* ago. When he'd taken a one-way trip to Nepal. It hadn't been scanned since, which only meant one thing: Phineas was still somewhere on the other side of *the world*. As I'm sure you can

guess, it was a pretty crushing blow to our case.

"Aw, man," Ernie sighed, sounding pretty disappointed. "I was so sure it was him. I thought I was finally developing my Spidey-senses!"

Suddenly, a flood of bright light crashed over us, and rolling my eyes, I turned to tell the chupacabras to cut it out already, when I saw that Carter was standing right next to me—and so was Pepe.

Uh-oh.

Two security guards were standing in the doorway of the DMV. One pointed at us and yelled, "YOU FIVE, DON'T MOVE!"

Naturally, we did exactly the opposite.

"And that's our cue to exit stage right!" I shouted as we all dove back into the tunnel.

We dashed through the tunnel, our flashlight beams bouncing off the rocky walls as we hauled nalgas! We came out by the strip mall and raced across the street, me looking over my shoulder and feeling another rush of panic-fueled adrenaline surge through me as I saw the two security guards come scrambling out of the ground behind us.

"Oh, great! They're fast!" I shouted.

"Jorge, c'mon!" Liza urged.

Our footsteps echoed off the blacktop as we flew across the moonbeam-streaked street toward the studio lot. When we reached the twenty-foot-tall chain-link fence that surrounded the studio, Pepe leapt it in a single Superman bound.

"Hey, we can't do that!" Ernie protested, sweat pouring off his face.

Carter grinned. "I got an idea!" Then he grabbed Liza and Ernie and flung them headfirst over the fence like they were a pair of Barbie dolls, and Pepe caught them on the other side like a couple of footballs. Oh man, that looked like so much fun!

"Me next!" I told the big guy, and then it was all hang time!

"Can we go again?" Ernie asked Carter when he'd joined us.

"Maybe later!" Liza hissed. "C'mon!"

The security guards were already unlocking the main gate, yelling at us to "FREEZE!" and "PUT YOUR HANDS UP!" when we turned and bolted into the shadows of the studio.

Carter and Pepe ran out ahead of us, trying all the stage doors, and it wasn't until we came to our place, Stage 21, that a door actually opened.

"¡Por aquí!" Carter hissed as the sound of the security guards' footsteps grew closer and closer. We snuck into the stage, and you would've thought we'd lost those two by darting out of sight, but we hadn't! They must've seen us go in, and they were right on our tails, their flashlight beams bouncing off the walls and high ceilings as they chased us through dense junglescapes and barren alien planets. We tried to blend in at an Old West saloon, but that didn't quite work, either.

No matter what we did we just couldn't shake these guys!

"What are we gonna do?!" Liza gasped as we ran past the scaffolding I'd set up with my dad.

Then it hit me. "I got it!"

It took some quick thinking—and some even quicker fingers!—but in about three shakes of a goat's tail, all five of us were in fly wire harnesses and hanging about thirty feet off the ground, hidden in shadow, trying not to giggle too loudly as we watched the two bloodhound security guards dash off out of the stage and into the night.

I just couldn't wipe the huge grin off my face. "Built this thing myself! Waachaa!"

CHAPTER 24

It had been a close call. A *very* close call. But we'd finally given those two payasos the old slip!

Just in case, though, we decided to hang out in the stage for a bit to give them time to get good and far away. As a bonus, Carter finally got to mess around on the "monkey bars."

When the coast was clear, meaning Carter and Pepe could no longer smell the guards, we made our way toward the side door. We figured if the guards were still watching the stage, they'd probably watch the front entrance and the back, which made door number three the winner.

We had just reached it and were slipping out into the cool Los Angeles night when I realized Carter wasn't with us. "Aw, man, where'd he go?" I said.

Liza peeked back through the door into the dark

hallway. "You don't think he went for a second round on the monkey bars, do you?"

I sighed. "Knowing Carter—*yeah*."

"Want me to go find him?" asked Pepe, with the sort of naughty, fangy grin that screamed, *I wanna go play on the monkey bars, too!*

Ha! No thanks. One chupacabra running wild inside the stage was way more than enough. "Nah, I'll go get him. The rest of you keep a lookout for those guards. BRB!"

Quickly, but as quietly as I could manage, I made my way back through the dark stage to the stunt area. But when I got there, the chupacabra was nowhere to be found!

"Carter!" I hissed into the shadows. "Carter, where are you?"

Nothing. You could've heard a pin drop in that place.

What is that big furball up to?

My first hunch was that his Hungry Hungry Hippo nose had led him to the catering tables, where there'd been a delicious spread of guava-and-cheese pastelitos this morning.

He's probably digging around in the trash can right

now for crumbs, I thought. But to my surprise, he wasn't there, either!

Suddenly, my Worry Meter was spiking into the red zone.

Where the heck had he gone? Just to be 100 percent sure, I took one more look around the monkey bars, and when I still didn't find him, I decided to get back to the others. Maybe Carter was back with them. Maybe I'd just missed him.

Only, as I was making my way through the offices, the figure of an enormous fanged monster suddenly leapt at me out of the dark!

"Jorge!" it hissed. Oh, thank God, it wasn't Count Dracula—it was Carter!

"DUDE, YOU SCARED THE PANTS OFF ME!" I whisper-roared. "WHERE WERE YOU?! AND WHAT IS *THAT*?"

I had just noticed a wide nylon bracelet on Carter's wrist. It looked like a high-tech dog collar, with a teeny blinking green light embedded deep in the material.

The big guy grinned down at it. "This? Issa friendship bracelet!"

"Oh. Who gave it to you?"

"Your abuelita."

"My *WHAT*? Why?"

"As a going-away present. Before we left for camp. She's very nice."

"She's not very nice! She's not nice at all! She didn't give *me* anything, and I'm her grandson!"

Carter shrugged like he didn't have an explanation for me.

"Okay, whatever. Answer my first question! Where were you? And you *better* not say playing hide-and-seek with a mouse!"

"No, I not playin', Jorge! I thought I heard somebody."

"Carter, you can't just wander off like that! It's okay in the woods back home, but definitely not here in L.A.!"

"But I heard something!" he hissed.

"Heard *what*?"

My eyes, suddenly feeling huge in my face, locked on Carter's. "Did you hear that?"

"Uh-huh! Is what I heard before!"

All of a sudden, a horrible wailing shriek ripped through the stage! You know those high-pitched, spine-tingling screams you hear in a lot of black-and-white horror movies? The kind that instantly turn your blood to ice and make all the little hairs on the back of your neck stand on end? Yeah, it was sort of like that. Only about a *bazillion* times scarier, because I knew it hadn't come from my TV speakers! If my eyes would've popped out any farther from my face, I would've looked like a human lobster as I swung my head up to look at Carter.

"What was that?" I gasped.

Looking puzzled, the chupacabra shook his head. He didn't have any clue, either. But I could see my mounting fear reflected in those enormous eyes.

"C'mon!" I said, and we both took off in the direction of the scream.

Now, I know what you're thinking: *Jorge! Why would you run toward a creepy horror movie scream in a dark, empty stage? Definitely not the smartest move.*

And I agree. It wasn't. But I did have the big guy to

back me up, and if I'd learned anything in this world, it's that you should always try to help those who need it. That's what being a good person is all about. And you should always try to be a good person.

Only, what I saw when we reached the big office at the far end of the hall left *me* wanting to scream for help...

For a moment, all I could think was *¡Dios mío! Sophie was right! There* was *a ghost in Stage 21!* But it was worse than that. It was waaay worse!

She'd been right about something else, too. This wasn't your average, everyday, run-of-the-mill haunted bedsheet. No. This, my amigos, was none other than *La Llorona*!

There was a lamp on in the office, and in its soft yellow glow, there was no mistaking her—not even from behind: that creepy, old-school bridal gown, dirty and blood streaked, rippling as if caught in a gust of wind; the long, jet-black hair tangled with leaves; the clawlike hands; the bone-thin arms and shrivel-y, leathery skin. A mist as dense and gray as sea fog hovered around her bare feet, and her toenails had grown out and twisted, over the centuries, into something like the talons of a vulture. She was a horrifying sight! Even worse than a geometry pop quiz!

Someone squeaked. Not gonna lie—it was probably me.

Next thing I knew, La Llorona's head snapped around and her gaze narrowed on us, sending the biggest *¡híjole!* chill of all time shivering down my spine! Her eyes were like two bottomless pits, and streaks of black tears flowed down her cheeks like liquid tar. Her face was paler than a full moon on Halloween.

Then La Llorona stretched a clawed hand toward us, and with a frame-cracking *bang*, the office door slammed shut in our faces. Before I could say anything, the chupacabra was already lunging toward it, hand stretched out, fangs bared. I knew what the big guy was thinking, because it was exactly what *I* was thinking: that La Llorona was the ghost Sophie the janitor had sensed. The ghost that was behind all the mysterious on-set disappearances.

And that she was about to nab herself another crew member! Still, did I think flexing on a mythical, über*terrifying* fantasma was a good idea? Heck no!

"CARTER, DON'T!"

But as he flung the door open and charged into the room, hissing and growling, sweeping his angry chupacabra gaze around, I saw that La Llorona had straight-up vanished. She was gone! And as I poked my head into the office to peek around, I saw that so was the hombre with the baseball cap. There was nobody in there. We were too late.

Another somebody had been kidnapped from Stage 21.

CHAPTER 25

"Let's go over it again from the beginning," Liza said back at Carter's apartment later that night. It was almost ten o'clock, and Pepe had already sped back home, hoping to arrive before his grandpa noticed he was gone and started suspecting things. Pepe still hadn't told him what Liza, Ernie, Carter, and I were actually doing here.

"Liza, there's nothing to go over!" I said, flopping down on the couch, an ice-cold pouch of Capri-Sun in my hand. "I already told you. We saw La Llorona! It's her!"

"Jorge, when people get into high-pressure situations, they see all sorts of things that aren't really there. It's a simple stress reaction. We don't know for sure *what* you saw."

"What do you mean you don't know for sure? *I* know for sure! And Carter was there! He told you he saw her, too!"

"Carter thought he saw Chester Cheetah in a bag of Cheetos once," she pointed out. (True story, by the way.) "He's not exactly what you would call a reliable witness. No offense," she said to Carter.

The big guy, who was sprawled out on a beanbag chair, pawing lazily through one of the million scripts that had piled up by the door, shrugged like he hadn't taken any. "Is okay," he told her. "I really did see Chester dat time."

Liza gave me a *See-what-I-mean?* look. "Jorge, we can't base an entire investigation on a 'ghost sighting.' That'd be totally unscientific. Besides, how would we even go about tracking down a ghost? And how would we catch it? It's not like we're the Ghostbusters, you know."

"All I can tell you is what we saw, Liza," I said. "It's La Llorona. I don't know who Pepe saw leaving the studio that night, but whoever it was, they're working with La Llorona. She's the kidnapper!"

"*Ghost*napper," Ernie corrected from the other

couch, where he was anxiously swiping around on a tablet, trying to find tips on how to avoid being kidnapped by incorporeal entities.

"Okay, *ghost*napper. Whatever! My point is," I said, "we heard a call for help, then we heard her trademark wailing cry, and then we saw *her* in one of the offices, right as she was probably kidnapping the man who called for help!"

"Except that you didn't *actually* see her kidnapping anybody," said Liza.

"No, but Sophie the janitor pretty much did. She saw the ghost in Mr. Ultio's office right when Robert went missing!"

"Sophie didn't see *anything*," Liza said with a frustrated groan.

"Yeah, she did! With the eyes of her mind, remember?"

"I'm still trying to forget," admitted Ernie, scrolling even faster on his tablet.

"But it's not even that much of a stretch!" I told Liza. "All her legends are about her kidnapping people! I'm telling you, she's the one behind all those missing people!"

"I not worried," Carter said happily from the beanbag chair. "Pepe said if it really is La Llorona haunting the stage, all he would have to do is find her kids—dat's all she really want—and she'll go away forever. He said he gonna find dem."

Liza ignored all that. Sighing, she sat down on the recliner across from me with her pencil in one hand and a bright red reporter's notepad in the other. "Fine. Let's say you *did* actually see a ghost, Jorge—"

"Which we definitely *did*."

"Sure. Now, think this through with me..." said Liza. "Why on earth would a wandering, vengeful spirit be targeting a specific cast and crew? Why is she only kidnapping people from Stage 21? And why only from Mr. Gomez's movie? You say she could be working with someone else, but why? What could a ghost gain from any of this?" When I couldn't provide a solid hypothesis, Liza said, "See? It doesn't make sense. A ghost—La Llorona or any other disembodied entity, for that matter—is missing the most critical element for any crime: a motive."

"Liza, a ghost wouldn't *need* a motive!" I told her. "She's La Llorona! She doesn't play by your silly rules, she does whatever she wants. Or maybe Sophie's right. Maybe she's mad because they're making a movie about her!"

"I don't buy it," said Liza. "This isn't even the first movie about her. Why didn't she kidnap people off those sets? It's just not adding up. It'd at least make some sense if she were kidnapping *kids* on set."

"*OH, C'MON!*" Ernie burst out. "Liza, you just jinxed it! Now she's definitely going to start kidnapping kids, and I just know *I'm going to be the first!*" He looked miserable now. Miserable and terrified. It was a sad combination.

Liza, ignoring him, reached a hand into her pocket. "And there's one more major strike against your La Llorona theory, Jorge. Remember this?" She held up Oscar's little golden head. "Explain to me how this ended up in the director's trailer office at the exact time of Robert Villegas's kidnapping. Do you think La Llorona collects infamous Hollywood memorabilia?"

Honestly, I didn't know what to think. I felt confused. And overwhelmed. And most of all, scared. Scared for Pepe and his clan. Scared for Mr. Gomez's movie and crew. Scared for my friends and me—and, believe it or not, scared for Manny, too. Because if Carter and I really *did* see what we thought we saw, then the four of us (and everybody else in Stage 21) were up to our necks in some serious ectoplasm.

"I don't know," I told her. "But I can't figure it out lying on this couch. I need some fresh air. I'm going for a walk."

Carter came with me. He said he didn't want me walking around L.A. all sad and alone, and I appreciated that. The bloodsucker had a heart of gold. He really did. And apparently, I wasn't the only one who thought so. About halfway up Sunset Boulevard, we saw this—

"Dude, is that a new one?" I gaped up at the billboard. "How many movies are you going to be in?"

He shrugged, smiling softly at me. "Math not my best subject." I guess that was a fair answer. It wasn't mine, either.

Under the hazy glow of traffic lights, we walked and walked and walked, winding our way deeper into the Mission Hills neighborhood of greater Los Angeles, my feet telling us when and where to turn. My brain wasn't involved. It didn't need to be. I knew these streets. I knew these sidewalks. They were my old friends. I'd grown up on them. I'd ridden my bike along their maze of concrete trails, my skateboard all the way down and across the San Fernando Valley. I'd busted up my elbow pretty bad on the corner of Van Nuys and Amboy. I'd smacked my first home run up in Brand Park. I knew this place like I knew the back of my own hand, and already I could feel that sweet whisper of home humming pleasantly in my ears. I let my feet lead us down all the familiar paths, and next thing I knew, I'd wound up on a sleepy stretch of sidewalk in front of the tiny restaurant, La Cocinita, where I used to sell my baseball cards on weekends to help my mom out with rent money, and where my mom still worked.

And there she was now... my mom in her waitress apron, looking so beautiful with her long, dark hair pulled back, her face tired and a little flushed, but a light in her eyes—the same light that kept her working jobs like this all over L.A. so she could put a roof over our heads and food on our table. Man, you had to appreciate moms like mine. They love us more than we'll ever know.

Standing there, it took everything in me not to go running in there and throw my arms around her and tell her how much I loved her and how bad I'd missed her.

I always talked to my mom about my problems. She was the one person I could always go to when I needed advice, because moms give the best advice.

I felt like I needed her now more than ever. I couldn't remember the last time I felt so confused—so mixed up inside. But I knew that I couldn't let myself take one more step toward that restaurant. If my mom saw me, she'd probably throw a fit (after crying a lot and kissing me on the head about fifty times, of course), and that would be the end of our case *and* of Pepe's woods. But I couldn't let that happen, because I knew what it was like to lose your home and I would do anything I could to keep those poor, peaceful creatures from losing theirs.

My mom had always been my rock. I'd never known anyone who was braver. But I would have to be brave myself now.

Happy that I'd gotten to see her, but also feeling my heart crumbling like pastelitos, I moved on, down the dark sidewalk.

CHAPTER 26

Carter didn't say much as we walked.

He was trying to give me a chance to sort out my feelings in my head.

He always knew when to say something and when to let me think. The goat-loving furball was pretty cool like that.

When my feet stopped again, I looked around and saw that we were standing in front of my house. It was where I'd been living with my mom before she sent me out to New Mexico. The place looked just how I remembered it, too—with the pink stucco walls, wrought iron window bars, and the Spanish tile roof that always shone in the moonlight.

Five minutes later, we were up in my favorite spot. The climb was even easier than the last time I'd made it.

"It looks like a giant silver dollar tonight," I told Carter.

"To me, it looks like a glowing wheel of magical goat cheese," said the chupacabra.

I didn't know if the moon really was made of magic cheese or not, but I knew that every time I sat up on a roof somewhere, watching it, my worries and anxieties just sort of melted away. The moon was always up there, always smiling down on me. Wherever I happened to be.

For a long time, there was only the croaking of tree frogs and the chirping of tiny crickets hiding out down in the sagebrush. Finally, Carter said, "Why you sad, Jorge?"

I shrugged. "I'm not as much sad as I am confused." Sometimes you can mix up confusion with anger. I'd learned that. That's why it's good to talk your feelings out.

"What are you confused about?" asked Carter. "Your dad?"

I blinked, surprised. "How'd you know?"

"Because I know you, Jorge. And because I see da way you look at him."

"Yeah, he's always been this big sore spot for me. And I only just met him the other day. I just..." *How do I say this?* "I just wish I understood why, that's all."

The chupacabra sounded confused. "Why what?"

"Why he left. Why he ran out on his own kid. Why he never came by once, not even to say hi. *Why?*"

"Ask 'im," said Carter, and I sighed, shaking my head. "I can't."

"Why not?"

"Because that's not something you can ask someone. He probably had a million and one reasons for doing it. And probably none would make any sense to me." Some questions didn't come with answers. And I guess we had to be okay with that.

We fell into silence again as the moon shone yellow and a warm breeze blew in off the faraway Pacific. "Your mom looks like a nice person," Carter whispered into the silence.

"She is," I said. "A great person. But I'm mad at her."

"Why?"

"Because she sent me away, remember?" Seeing her in the restaurant tonight had brought it all back. That whole terrible day. The whole week up to her *tossing* me out of my own house. "I know that's also the reason I met you and Liza and Ernie, and I don't regret any of that, obviously. But I can't figure her out again. If you really love someone—I mean, like, *really* love them—how can you just throw them out like yesterday's pizza? How could you send them to live a million miles away from you? It doesn't make any sense."

"Jorge, remember what I told you before," whispered Carter. "It's *because* she loves you that she sent you away."

And suddenly, I realized I was crying. I didn't even mean to. The tears had just come, streaking down my face now, cold on my burning cheeks. "You're going to have to explain that one again to me, buddy. 'Cause I'm just not seeing it right now..."

I felt the chupacabra's big hand on my back. The pads of his paws were soft against my shoulder. He said, "I know 'xactly how you feel, Jorge."

"How?"

"The day me and my family were attacked in the woods, remember? By los dips. The vampire dogs. They chased us and chased us, and when I didn't feel like I could run no more, my mom say, 'Carter, we must split up. I go one way. You go the other. Is the only way we will survive.' She told me, 'Carter, run! Run and don't stop running until you find a very, very tall tree!' That's the tree I found by your grandparents' house. Where I was hiding, scared and all alone, when you found me. My mom sent me away, too, Jorge. She sent me away, not because she didn't love me, but *because* she loved me. My mom saved my life. I am here today because of what my mom did. And even though we apart, I still see her smiling down on me every night."

Just then there was a *click* and I heard the screech of a door opening. A wedge of light spilled across the front lawn of the house as Carter and I ducked down behind the slope of the roof, just our eyeballs peeking out.

Somebody had come out of the house. It was my mom, I realized with a jolt of surprise. She must've walked home and gone inside without us even noticing. She was squinting up toward the roof now, in the dark, like she was searching for something.

Suddenly, our next-door neighbor opened her front door and poked her head out, asking, "You okay, Linda? Something wrong?"

"No, nothing, Raquel. Thank you. I just thought I heard my little boy up there. He used to love to sit out on the roof at night. I was always having to bring him down. I miss him so much it hurts," she said.

CHAPTER 27

So the big guy might've had a point. Maybe we didn't understand all the stuff our parents did for us and maybe we never would. But most of the time, I guess, it was for our own good.

Being back home and seeing my mom (not to mention my dad, for the first time ever) had put my feelings in a spin cycle.

But Carter had helped me figure things out a little.

I know it's pretty weird to pour your heart out to a seven-foot-tall, blood-slurping monster, but what can I say? That was my life. And this bloodsucking monster happened to be a pretty wise dude.

Anyway, by the time the fur-covered movie star and I got back to the apartment, Liza had already come up with our next move. That didn't really surprise me since she was a plan-making wizard. But what did surprise me was that the idea had been Ernie's, and that he'd gotten it just a little while ago marathoning old *Star Trek* episodes.

The idea was this: stop looking for the villain and start *watching* the victims.

Let's face it—Carter and I were strongly on Team Llorona. We'd both seen her. With our own ojos. Now, did that mean she was behind the vanishings? Not necessarily. Even though it was my *strong* suspicion that she was. Liza, however, wasn't ever going to buy that. She was a woman of science. She'd need proof that La Llorona was more than just some urban legend, and that she'd been in the studio, and that she actually had something to do with the vanishings. And she kind of had a point—technically, we hadn't *actually* her seen kidnap anyone.

But that was the genius behind Ernie's idea. It didn't really matter who (or what) any of us believed was behind the vanishings. Going forward, our sole focus was to be there (and ready) when the next one happened, so we could crack this case once and for all.

We already had the perfect way to do it, too. Pepe's list! We knew exactly who the next victim was going to be. We'd known it from the very beginning. Liza was more than a little annoyed with herself that she hadn't thought of this before, but I told her not to sweat it, that nobody's perfect. Though she came awfully close sometimes.

The following morning, we put our plan into action. The next name on Pepe's list was Eduardo Cruz, the movie's leading man, and we came up with a strategy to keep a round-the-clock eye on him while he was on studio property. It's where all the vanishings had taken place, so we figured that should more than do the trick.

Only . . . a teeny, tiny monkey wrench had been tossed into our finely tuned plan: Eduardo the superstar actor had been declared missing as of this morning!

It was the director himself, Mr. Ultio, who called us into his office to spill the deets. Mr. Ultio was a big, burly dude with a deeply wrinkled face and bright little eyes that didn't seem to match the rest of him. The backs of his hands were almost as hairy as Carter's.

> Judging from everything we know, what we can see on our cameras, Eduardo went missing sometime late last night, right here in the studio.

"That was his cry for help that Carter and I heard!" I hissed to Liza. "Then La Llorona nabbed him! I don't want to rub it in or whatever, but . . . I told you, I told you, I TOLD YOU!"

"This doesn't prove anything, Jorge!" she hissed back. "Now let me listen to what Mr. Ultio has to say!"

His face grave, the director dude went on. "I'm taking it upon myself to make everyone in the cast and crew aware of these mysterious happenings. I know you three just started working here and might not have heard, but this isn't the first disappearance in Stage 21. It's happened before and I'm afraid it can happen again. I thank you three dearly for volunteering to help us with our movie, but if I were you, I'd quit while you still can." The ominous tremble in that deep baritone of Mr. Ultio's almost made me want to take his advice.

But Vegan Sherlock had a few questions. "Mr. Ultio," said Liza, "do you have any idea what Eduardo was doing in the studio after hours?"

The director's wrinkly face became grave and he nodded once, very slowly and very solemnly, twirling a pencil between his thick fingers. "I do ... because *I* told him to come here."

Ernie and I exchanged confused looks. "What do you mean you told him to come here?" Ernie asked with a slight tremor in his voice.

Mr. Ultio, sinking gradually back in his chair, pointed the pencil at the velvet-covered necklace box on his desk. "I received a strange call while I was out of town last night. A tip, warning me that some of our on-set valuables were in danger. Specifically, that necklace right there. One of our actresses wears it in about ten percent of her scenes, and it's worth a tidy sum. So I called Eduardo, our leading man, who's the only other person who knows the combination to the on-set safe, and asked him to retrieve the necklace and take it home with him for safekeeping."

"Was the necklace stolen?" Liza asked.

Mr. Ultio shook his head. "No. It's right there in that box."

"Did you recognize the voice? The one that called you."

"No. Unfortunately, I did not. I tried to have my phone company trace the number, but it was blocked. For what it's worth, the voice was a woman's."

"La Llorona!" Ernie gasped under his breath.

Liza snuck a glare at him. "I don't think ghosts make phone calls, Ernie," she whispered.

"So, what do you think is going on?" I asked Mr. Ultio.

The old man let out a long, tired sigh. "I can't afford to think about that. We do have footage of a group of hooligans running around in costume inside this stage last night. A little while after Eduardo came in. Maybe they have something to do with the phone call about the necklace or the disappearances, though we didn't catch them doing anything nefarious on camera."

Not sure why, but I had this sneaking suspicion

that I knew those costumed "hooligans," and they definitely didn't have anything to do with that phone call or the disappearances.

Good thing none of us ever took our masks off! I thought with a huge sigh of relief, glancing over at Ernie again.

"That most recent footage aside," Liza said quickly, trying to move smoothly past the uncomfortable subject, "what do you believe has been going on?"

Running a weary hand through his thick head of hair, Mr. Ultio said, "I say it's a hoax."

Ernie blinked at him. "A hoax?"

"Why not?" said Mr. Ultio. "That's what the police believe."

"So you contacted the police, too?" Liza asked, I guess remembering that Sophie had also contacted them.

"Of course! The missing people's families are devastated, as you can imagine, and I feel some responsibility, since it's my movie. The police have seen our other security camera footage, how the missing people go into rooms without any windows or doors and then mysteriously vanish. There are no cameras in the rooms themselves, but we can clearly see cast or crew going into various rooms and never coming out. There is no logical explanation, so the police arrived at the only logical conclusion: that we're all pulling some kind of elaborate hoax for publicity. With the premise of our movie being what it is and a title like *The Curse of La Llorona*, you can understand their suspicions. It wouldn't be the first time a publicity stunt along those lines has been tried around here."

A little of the boy-who-cried-wolf effect, I thought.

"But you're not pulling any kind of hoax," said Liza.

"No." The director shrugged. "But that doesn't mean some of the cast might not be."

"I really don't think they are," I told Mr. Ultio.

He nodded like he agreed with me. "Maybe not. But there's nothing else to think. I can't let myself believe anything else, in hopes that they're safe."

"Why haven't you considered postponing production?" Liza asked. "I know *The Desert Rose* was postponed for a few months and everything was fine."

At the mention of that idea, or maybe that movie, Mr. Ultio snapped the pencil he'd been playing with clean in half. He looked like he'd had a sudden violent muscle spasm.

I guess Ernie also noticed this, because he said, "Uh, you okay, Mr. Ultio?"

The burly director dude nodded several times like he was slowly pulling himself together. "I'm fine. Just please don't mention that movie to me. I had a dear friend in the running for an award that it won." He drew in a deep breath. "But to answer your other question, yes, I have considered it," he told Liza. "But I simply cannot. Can you imagine if I were to shut down production because cast and crew were vanishing in an impossible manner right off the set? Throw in rumors of ghosts in the stage, and I'd be the laughingstock of directors everywhere! This is my first movie. It took me *months* to convince Mr. Gomez that I was the right director for the job," he confided. "Worse, if I shut down now, Mr. Gomez is *finished*! I don't know if you are aware, but this movie is his last chance to save his production company. If we can't get this wrapped and out in theaters quickly, it's over! Mr. Gomez is a nice man. He does a lot of good with his company. I can't let him go out like that. Which means that I *must* get this movie across the finish line!"

CHAPTER 28

Things were getting dicey around here, and *fast*.

With Eduardo's Houdini impersonation last night, the disappearances were happening closer and closer together, and there were exactly two more to come.

The *last* two.

Mr. Gomez, the owner of the production company.

And Manny Martinez, none other than my pops. Who just so happened to be the next batter up.

We were now juggling the fates of people, companies, and even relatives. ¡Órale! I'd never felt so much pressure in my entire life!

The only good thing, I guess, was that Manny wasn't going to be hard to keep an eye on. I was his assistant, so I had a built-in excuse to stick close to the guy.

Which was exactly what I did, all through that morning, from the second he set foot on the set.

Only I might have been sticking a little *too* close, because Manny had started to notice...

A little after lunch, Manny heard the unmistakable call of nature, and I slumped tiredly down in the cushy chair next to the restroom, thinking, *Ah, finally! Halftime!*

Only it didn't take very long for the ref to blow the second-half whistle. I'd had my eyes shut for less than *two* minutes when I heard a rush of pounding sneakers and looked around to see Liza and Ernie hurrying this way. They were huffing and puffing like the Big Bad Wolf.

"Jorge, what are you doing?!" Liza demanded breathlessly.

I shook my head. "Nothing. Why?"

"Because I look over and don't see Manny anywhere! Where is he??"

I jerked a thumb over my shoulder. "Relax. He's sitting on the porcelain throne."

"But why aren't you in there with him?" she snapped. "You're never supposed to let him out of your sight!"

"Liza, what do you want me to do?" I snapped back. "Follow him into the stall?!"

"Don't you get it, Jorge?" she hissed. "All these

people have been kidnapped when they're by *themselves*. We have to have eyes on him even in the bathroom in case the kidnapper makes their move!"

¡Órale! She kind of had a point there. "All right, all right," I told Liza. "I'll wait in the stall next to his and at least try to keep *an ear* on him." I sighed. "He already thinks I'm weird, just wait until I try to make potty talk with h—"

A terrible shriek from the bathroom suddenly cut me off! My heart stopped. Four pairs of eyes bugged and stared in frozen terror at each other.

"Oh no!" gasped Ernie.

That's when Carter spotted it—or smelled it, or something!

"Jorge, ¡mira!" he cried, pointing at the floor in a panic. My eyes swung down, and I saw, to my total shock, tendrils of vapory mist creeping out from the slot under the door.

The mist curled gently up like fumes, then vanished, white and steamy, into the cool stage air. I recognized that mist. It was the same one Carter and I had seen last night.

It was La Llorona's mist!

Liza's eyes, suddenly full of fear, locked on mine. "Your dad's being kidnapped right now!" she screamed.

There wasn't a second to waste. We charged into the bathroom like a SWAT team, Carter nearly tearing the door off its hinges. Then swirls of mist were slithering around our sneakers like snakes as we skidded into the big white-tiled rectangle of the bathroom.

Only . . . there was nobody there! Nobody at the row of shiny sinks, nobody at the urinals! Thinking fast, Ernie and I went stall by stall, kicking in the doors, but when we reached the last one in the row, we saw that the king had abdicated his throne.

Translation: the place was empty!

"But this is *impossible*!" I shouted. "Where could he have gone?" Then I remembered that *all* the vanishings had been impossible. That's why this case was a total head scratcher!

Carter whirled around to face us. "What we gonna do?"

Fortunately, E-dog was all over it. "Follow the mist!"

"That's right!" I said as the genius of it hit me. "Follow the mist, find the ghost!" It had a weird sort of logic to it. Kind of like multiplication tables.

"Exactly!" shouted Ernie, pumping his fist. Then, a split second later, I guess the implications of the whole "find the ghost" part finally dawned on him.

CHAPTER 29

Imagine following a vanishing trail of the lightest, mistiest vapor through a twenty-thousand-foot-plus stage busy with movie people trying to make a movie.

If that seems kind of hard to do, that's because it is. In fact, it would've been downright *impossible* with only three sets of regular human eyes. Good thing for us, we had an extra pair. And they happened to be an extra-large, extra-*sharp* pair of chupacabra eyes!

Bent over, eyes down, our faces only inches from the gray linoleum floors like a pack of trained bloodhounds picking up a scent, we tracked the slowly dissolving ghost mist around corners and across sets, between table legs and people legs, into rooms, out of rooms, down hallways, over props and prop masters, across a catwalk, and just barely past a catering table loaded with piles of freshly powdered jelly doughnuts that had the big guy's mouth watering with their sugary, slurpy, blood-like centers. Then we hit a sort of dead end—the door to Mr. Ultio's personal trailer. One quick scan of the mess of signs hanging from it gave us a pretty good idea how he felt about uninvited guests. And it wasn't exactly a warm and fuzzy feeling.

"When it's closed, that means he's busy," I said, remembering what Emmet had told me. "Probably editing the movie script or something."

"Sorry, but our script is going to reach its grand

finale way faster than his!" Liza said. She gave Carter the go-ahead nod, and he gave the door the kind of yank that could've ripped the trunk off an elephant—except somehow the door didn't budge!

"It must be super-reinforced titanium!" Ernie gasped. "Like the *Enterprise*!"

"We've got to get inside!" Liza shouted. "For all we know, Archie Gomez is in there with him, and could be getting kidnapped as we speak! Remember, his is the last name on the list!"

¡Órale! She had a point!

But how we were supposed to get into Mr. Ultio's trailer?!

"Looking for this?" said a familiar voice.

The four of us whirled around to see Albert Lee, Carter's agent, holding up a key and grinning like the cat who ate the last sardine. The key was this big silver job—like the kind that would open a treasure chest. "You want in on this movie, don't ya, big guy?" he said to Carter.

The chupacabra looked confused. He glanced slowly between Liza and me, then turned back to Albert and just sort of shrugged like, *Yeah, I guess*.

"C'mon, I'm your agent!" said Albert, grinning.

"You don't have to play coy with me!" His eyes flicked past us to Mr. Ultio's trailer and a look of determination filled his face. "You want to talk to the director about a lead role, and he's stonewalling you, isn't he?"

Carter blinked and shrugged again.

"I knew it!" shouted Albert. "See, I can sense these things! Listen to me, Carter, you're the perfect man for whatever role you're trying to get, and I'm not just saying that because I'm your agent. You need this movie and this movie needs you! The four of you are going in that trailer right now, you're going to see Mr. Ultio, and you are not taking no for an answer!"

CHAPTER 30

Once we got the door open, we flew into Mr. Ultio's trailer office, looking around at the mess of manuscripts and stacked books. I couldn't see Mr. Ultio, because his high-back leather chair was spun around facing the opposite wall. The mist, meanwhile, cut right through the middle of the trailer, though it was very faint now, and hard to see.

"Carter, can you still follow it?" I asked, panting with nerves, and the big guy gave me a thumbs-up.

"Mr. Ultio, Manny Martinez has just gone missing!" Liza was saying as she approached his big desk. "And we believe your producer, Archie Gomez, will be—"

But as she reached his desk, the words still dangling off her lips, we got another surprise. "He's not here!" Liza shouted, spinning the empty chair around. "La Llorona might've kidnapped him, too!"

Carter was down on all fours in front of a huge bookshelf in the back corner. He hissed, "Da mist go under dere!"

"Then we've got to go under there, too!" I shouted.

One push from a chupacabra was all it took, and the bookshelf slid smoothly aside to reveal—¡híjole!—a secret, shadowy passageway cut right into the trailer wall!

"Please don't tell me we have to go in there," whispered Ernie with an audible gulp.

"I won't tell you, but we've still got to," said Liza.

"Carter, lead the way," I hissed, and the seven-foot-tall bloodsucking scaredy-cat frowned.

"But why me, Jorge?"

"Because you're the only one who could drink a Slurpee from across a room!" In case you're wondering, I was referring to his *enormous* Dracula fangs. "Now go!"

Silently, cautiously, we followed the big guy into the narrow pitch-dark tunnel. Our hoarse breathing echoed off the walls as we shuffled along sideways for a few feet until we came to a sort of creepy corridor.

It looked like some giant storage closet for all the creepiest movie props—decapitated mannequins, creepy clown masks, prop butcher knives covered with fake blood, you name it.

"Yeah, but what is this place?" Liza said uneasily.

Ernie's eyes lit up. "Oh! I think this is the alley between Stage 21 and 22. It used to be Stage 23, a smaller soundstage. But it nearly burned down about a decade ago, and they just expanded Stages 21 and 22 to take up the space. I guess you could say this is what's left."

Liza and I both stared at him like, *Seriously? How do you know that?*

Ernie shrugged. "What? I was reading up on some Hollywood history."

We wandered farther in, and the props and posters started becoming more and more specific, especially a whole bunch of stuff marked with the name of that famous *Desert Rose* movie. There were tons of posters of Eduardo Cruz with his name crossed out, as well as cast posters used as bull's-eyes on the walls, with knives sticking out of them and spray paint all over the place.

"Can someone say 'disturbing' . . . ?" I just wasn't sure what else you even *could* say.

All of a sudden, the whole alley seemed to open up, and now we were in some huge enclosed space that looked like the result of a headfirst collision between three different movie sets. To our right, and partially blocked by a wall, was what looked like the set of a high school science class—I could see a tall metal shelf loaded with beakers and Bunsen burners, and the right side of the periodic table poster up on the wall. To our left was what looked like the back of a performing stage, a huge black curtain hanging from the ceiling, stacks of crates loaded with old costumes, and a couple flights of wooden steps leading right into a brick wall.

Way off in the distance, toward the back of the space where it widened out, I could see what looked like a woodsy scene, complete with a forest of ten-foot-tall artificial willow trees and a big shimmery lake in the middle. It was the oddest thing. Almost as if a half acre of wild woods had grown out of a backlot alley. Kind of cool, actually.

Then we discovered something else...

I picked up the prosthetic chin and wig. "It looks just like Mr. Ultio," I whispered, trying to wrap my head around all this nuttiness.

"And this one has the same hair and ears as Lola," said Liza.

"And dat one like Emmet." Carter pointed.

"Oh no!" Ernie gasped, his brown eyes huge with terror as he clutched Carter's arm. "The ghost has chopped them all into little pieces!"

Liza and I turned to glare at him. "These are *fake*, Ernie. Fake skin, hair, and noses," Liza told him.

E-dog blinked. "Oh."

But what does this all mean? I couldn't help wondering.

Behind the table, on a low stack of crates near the wardrobe rack, I found a small wooden treasure chest—something off the set of a pirate movie. Curiosity got the best of me, so I flipped up the latch, carefully lifted the lid, and what I saw had a big old question mark forming right between my gaping eyes. It was a chest of . . . *passports*? There must've been close to twenty different ones—from all over the world. Switzerland to Argentina, and everywhere in between. The names inside were all different, too.

But as I flipped through them, I kept seeing the exact same face in the picture box. Sure, slight variations here and there. Sometimes he was blond, sometimes he had a beard, a couple of times he wore glasses.

Liza had been peering over my shoulder, and—no big surprise—I could see all my anxiousness and nerves reflected on her eerily lit face. "What is going on?" she whispered.

"Hear dat?" hissed Carter, turning toward the web of shadows out ahead of us.

I really didn't hear anything, but then again, I didn't have the ears of an apex predator. Silently, sticking close together now, we made our way deeper into this gloomy backstage world, following the big guy, me holding tightly on to the scaly end of his tail while Liza and Ernie held on to the way shorter and way-less-scaly tail of my T-shirt.

As we rounded a corner, edging past a dusty old circus decoration—a giant plaster clown face, it looked like—a rush of bright light and movement stabbed our eyes!

Ernie spoke for everyone when he let out a champagne-glass-shattering shriek, and the four of us jumped back as our collective hearts jumped into our collective throats!

A flashlight! I thought. But nope—it wasn't a flashlight. It was a movie projector!

And when I turned, I saw it was projecting a movie onto the bare cinder block wall we'd just crossed in front of, the flickering white light bright as fireworks in the gloom of the pitch-black room.

After we silently watched the film for a minute, it dawned on me that it wasn't a real movie being shown. It looked more like an award show.

"It's some kind of ceremony," I whispered, eyes glued to the picture. Tons of people in fancy dresses and tuxedos. Enormous red velvet curtains framed the gilded stage area that sort of reminded me of the Dolby Theatre in Hollywood.

"It's *the* award ceremony," said Liza, instinctively bringing the golden head out of her pocket. "That's the Oscars from a few years ago. The year that *The Desert Rose* took home Best Picture and Actor in a Leading Role."

She was right! The host had just called out the movie, and here came Eduardo Cruz onstage to accept his award. The next minute or so played out just how Mr. Gomez had described it to us over lunch: Phineas Alcaraz leaping onto the stage after Eduardo, snatching the award away with a violent, furious jerk, then making his angry speech before decapitating the Oscar and running off with the little golden noggin as security stormed the stage.

The scene cut out, then started playing again. The projector was on a loop.

As I stood there, feeling a slithering sort of creepiness begin to snake its way up my legs, I became aware of a strange sound—or was it *sounds*?—somewhere close by.

Listen! There in the background, just below the rattle of the movie projector . . . it sounded like, *Mmmm! Mmmhmm! Mmmhm mmm mmmhmm!*

"You hear that?" I asked, looking up at Carter.

The big guy nodded. "I see dem, too." One furry clawed finger was pointing toward the heavy shadows around and behind the movie projector. And when my straining eyes finally managed to penetrate those shadows, the world felt like it came to a shrieking halt!

CHUPACARTER AND THE CURSE OF LA LLORONA

CHAPTER 31

I almost couldn't believe my eyes! There was everybody, all the missing cast and crew! Even my dad! If I didn't know any better—and if there weren't gags and ropes binding their wrists and legs to the desks—I might've thought it was a night school class for adults.

Obviously, we were all too shocked to say anything. But then we got an even *bigger* shock when a voice spoke out of the dark: "I believe you have something that belongs to me."

I had no idea who had said that, because everyone that I could see was gagged. Maybe there was a ventriloquist in the group?

Turns out, there wasn't. It hadn't been any of them.

A second later, a figure melted out of a dark corner behind us. A man, tall and slim, thin lips pulled back in a vicious smile, wearing a fancy tux-and-scarf combo.

Sleek purple gloves covered his hands, and his dark leather shoes were so polished you could practically see our terrified, bug-eyed expressions in them.

I may not have been into the kind of movies he made, but I'd seen that sleek ferret-like face enough times over the past few days to know exactly who he was.

"You're Phineas Alcaraz!" Liza gasped, pointing an accusing finger at the guy.

A look of glowing satisfaction filled the world-famous thespian's face. His fingers fiddled excitedly with the silky red scarf draped around his neck as he said grandly, "Ah, so you recognize me! My, what astute youths! Is it from *The Little Merman*?"

I frowned. "What? No."

"Then it must be from *Casaroja*?"

Liza, Ernie, Carter, and I all glanced around at each other, shaking our heads.

"Nah," said Ernie. "We must've missed that one."

"Then perhaps you saw my triumphant performance in *Silence of the Clams*?"

"*Silence of the Clams*? I've never even heard of it," I admitted. "And, by the way, that's an awful title for a movie. Clams are *always* silent. They don't have vocal cords."

Anger flashed in the depths of those icy-blue eyes. "You filthy scoundrel! How dare you insult such a masterpiece?! It was nominated for five Academy Awards!"

"You're a *kidnapper* and a *saboteur*, and you're calling *him* a scoundrel?" asked Liza. "Excuse me, but I think somebody needs to take a look in the mirror."

The pointy end of Phineas's chinny-chin-chin rose a little higher as he shot us a snooty, condescending look. "Those things are not as terrible as you make them sound, really. I've played characters ten times as bad!"

"Yeah, except this isn't some TV miniseries—it's *real life*!" I pointed out.

Phineas grinned viciously around at us. "All the world's a stage, is it not?" Then, off our silence, he sneered, "Surely you brats have heard of William Shakespeare?"

Of course we had. But just to really stick it to the twerp, I said, "Shakes-*who*? It's not really ringing a bell."

The result was pretty funny, too. Ever seen the face a dog makes while trying to eat a lemon? It was something like that.

"Oh, what *vile* little wretches!" he huffed and puffed, and nearly blew us all down. "To be so unaware of the Bard? You need to be taken out of your ignorant misery. And while I'll admit you four snoops were a plot twist I did not see coming, this will most definitely be your *final* act!"

"Wait, you're going to kill us?" Ernie shrieked. I guess that was a plot twist that *he* hadn't seen coming.

"Unfortunately, you've left me little choice," Phineas said in an almost gloomy tone, "seeing as you've taken a behind-the-scenes peek into my grand scheme."

"Yeah, we saw your little makeup area back there," I said.

Ernie tsked at him. "Impersonating Lola, Emmet, and Mr. Ultio? That's *sooo* rude."

"I wasn't impersonating anyone, you buffoon," snapped Phineas. "I *am* them! Lola, Emmet, and Mr. Ultio are *my* characters! I made them up!"

Oh man, that explained a lot, actually! It also proved how great an actor this dude was!

"The idea was simple enough," he gloated. "By creating these characters, I could in effect infiltrate each department of the production and keep my ear close to the rumor mill. In the unlikely event someone saw something they shouldn't have, or began working out my scheme, I could react instantly, make the necessary adjustments, and avoid any unnecessary hiccups. Of course, I also used my characters to help fan the flames of fear throughout the cast, quite the enjoyable experience, if I do say so myself."

"You're really something else," I said.

"I'll take that as a compliment," he shot back. "Time to wrap. Any last words?"

"Yeah, my last words are that my buddy is about to put a world-class beatdown on you," I said. "See, while you spent your life working on your dramatic timing and delivery, my friend over here's been swinging around on trees and chasing wild goats. He could probably pick you up and snap you like a twig. So why don't you save the drama for your mama and just surrender to us?"

No sooner had I said that than Carter stepped protectively in front of us. His claws were out and his eyes had narrowed to smoldering little slits. He reminded me of a fur-covered Wolverine. The way things were going with his career, he probably *would* be cast in the next X-Men movie.

From deep in the chupacabra's throat, a low growl rumbled. "You not gonna hurt my friends..."

"Silence, over-actor!" erupted Phineas. "Oh yes... I've watched a few of your recent 'rehearsals.' And I am *unimpressed*, to say the least! My, has the profession gone downhill since my departure. In fact, you might be the most *unconvincing* monster I've ever laid eyes on! Even your costume is a complete farce!"

We all kind of looked around at each other like, *Seriously?*

"It couldn't look more fake!" roared Phineas. Then, quickly pulling himself together: "However, I am merely the brains of this organization. It's time for you to meet my *muscle* ... Oh, Rosalia!" he called in an annoying singsong voice.

Then, suddenly, from between the rows of fake trees out there by the lake, I saw something. A ghostly mist shimmering through the air.

Then the mist began to come together ... and to my horror, I saw an *actual* ghost materialize out of the shadows of a huge willow tree!

"It can't be ..." whispered Ernie in terror.

But as the thickening mist formed her weeping eyes and mouth, which was frozen in a scream, there was ZERO doubt about it.

It was La Llorona!

CHAPTER 32

"She really does exist!" Liza gasped.

"This is *another* one of those times I *really* don't like saying I told you so!" I whispered.

"Rosalia, get those brats!" snapped Phineas, and *that*, my friends, was our cue to exit stage left.

"¡CORRAN!" I shouted.

But not even an Olympic-gold-medal-winning sprinter could have gotten away in time. The four of us had only just turned to hightail it out of there when I heard that terrible ghostly shriek again, and La Llorona blurred up behind us, reappearing right on our nalgas! It happened that fast. One second she was on the other side of the lake, thirty yards away, and the next—*WHOOSH!*—she was snatching us all off our feet by the backs of our shirts (and by the fur, in Carter's case), as if we weighed nothing at all!

"Drown those vermin!" cried Phineas, and La Llorona glided us over to the lake while we kicked and screamed, struggling uselessly against the iron grip of those phantom fingers!

"Please think of another way to kill us!" I screeched. "The chupacabra is terrified of water!" Weak sauce, I know. But it was the first thing that came to my head.

Carter glanced at me, confused. "No, I'm not, Jorge."

"Dude, you're not helping!"

"I want my mommy!" Ernie was bawling.

"And I want the Ghostbusters!" I shrieked.

"Guys, please stop embarrassing yourselves!" shouted Liza. "At least die with some dignity!"

La Llorona already had dragged us into the water, almost in the middle of the lake, and once you were hanging over it, you could see that the water was WAAAY deeper than it had looked from the other side of the alley—at least twelve feet deep!

"CARTER, DO SOMETHING!" I shrieked, but the big guy was already trying his best, slashing and clawing at La Llorona's ghostly form and doing exactly *zero* damage. You just couldn't hurt her!

The legendary ghoul started the dunking process.

Next second, the four of us were flailing and splashing wildly around like a gang of water-hating Chihuahuas during bath time.

It's OVER! I thought. We were total goners! And I didn't even get a chance to tell my mom I loved her!

But there was still a chance to say something nearly as important to my friend. It was officially time to come clean...

"Ernie!" I screeched.

"Yeah?" he screeched back.

"I have a confession to make! You know that strawberry Pop-Tart that went missing in your room a couple of weeks ago?"

"Yeah?"

"It wasn't Carter who ate it. It was *me!*"

"JORGE, HOW COULD YOU?!" he screamed. "You know that's my favorite flavor! And it was my LAST one!"

"You two CANNOT be for real!" I heard Liza shout.

Suddenly, an image of my soon-to-be tombstone flashed before my eyes:

JORGE LOPEZ, AGE 12

MURDERED BY LA LLORONA

YES, REALLY!

I'm not going to lie—I was having a little trouble wrapping my brain around the fact that I was about to be drowned by the baddest, most vengeful people-drowning ghost in ALL of Mexican folklore! Though it was almost kind of cool, if you think about it.

Well, besides the being drowned part. I could definitely do without that.

SCREEEEE! Just then my eardrums were sucker punched by this huge screech of metal.

Whipping my head around and catching my breath, I saw giant slashes appear in the wall to our right. The aluminum screeched and sparked like someone was cutting through it with a buzz saw as even more slashes appeared, forming a sort of square shape.

And next thing I knew—*WHAM!*—that whole square section of the wall fell in with a huge crash! Harsh white light flooded in through the hole, followed by blacked-out silhouettes—at least a dozen of them—leaping into view. At first I thought they were people . . . but the way they moved was too fast and nimble. First dips, then a haunted piñata, then ghosts . . . what supernatural creature was coming after us now?

Then I saw what they were! I was hoping for

Ghostbusters, but we got even something better: *CHUPACABRAS!*

It was Pepe and his friends! His abuelo, too! They poured in, two and three at a time, fangs bared, claws out and looking about as deadly as any samurai sword.

They slashed their way through the wall! I realized with a surge of relief and surprise. They'd come to save us! Only... as powerful as they were, how could they fight a ghost?

"Ha! You think a bunch of furballs can defeat the most fearsome ghost in all legend?" Phineas roared defiantly.

"Never underestimate chupacabras!" Pepe's grandfather shot back. "And you should know that our kind only fights when it is *absolutely* necessary."

Phineas snorted. "If you believe you can reason with her, you're delusional." He turned to La Llorona. "Destroy them all!" he commanded.

With an otherworldly scream, La Llorona heaved us upward for another plunge into the icy water to finish us off, once and for all. From that height, I managed to catch sight of something completely unexpected.

From behind the wise old chupacabra's right leg, a little button-nosed face peeked shyly out. A human face. A little girl's face. But that wasn't the part that had me staring, had my jaw hanging somewhere around my belly button.

It was the fact that I could see right through her!

She was a ghost!

From behind Carlos's left leg, another little face peeked out. A boy's face, this time. And, in case you were wondering, he was also very clearly un fantasma.

"¿Mamá?" said the little girl in a whispery, echoing voice, looking at La Llorona.

"Mamá, ¿eres tú?" asked the little boy, sounding just as ghostly.

You could barely hear those two over all our splashing and shouting, but La Llorona's head snapped immediately toward their voices. I felt her entire body tense.

Then, in a single sudden motion, she lifted us out of the water and flung us out to the shallow part of the lake, where we landed on our heinies, coughing our lungs out!

"Anita? Juanito?" Her ghostly voice cracked with emotion and her ghostly white face had become even paler somehow.

Next thing I knew, the two little ghost kids raced out from behind Pepe's grandfather and came running over the lake to wrap their arms around their terrifying mother's legs.

La Llorona—no big surprise—burst out in huge, wailing sobs that tore through the alley so loudly and so hauntingly that I was surprised it didn't peel the posters off the walls.

It was a full-on ghostly reunion. Two ghost kids and their kid-snatching, lake-haunting mamá. It was almost sweet in a super spooky and sad sort of way.

From the other side of the alley, I saw Pepe wink at me. "Told you chupacabras can find anything, Jorge!"

I was almost too shocked to speak. Blinking water out of my eyes, I managed, "But how did you find them?"

"We had to visit every haunted house, cemetery, and Chuck E. Cheese in twelve states," revealed Pepe. "They were in the Albuquerque Chuck E. Cheese."

"He *never* knew where your children were," Pepe's grandpa told La Llorona. "That two-footer is an imposter! He dressed up as your husband to trick you!"

Dressed up as her husband? Oh! That must've been the "time-traveling mariachi" dude Pepe had followed into the woods that night! It had been Phineas in costume!

Man, Pepe's grandpa was a pretty sharp cat—er, *chupacabra*.

The world's greatest actor sneered viciously at him. "That's not true!"

But Pepe was already sniffing around, hound dog nose to the dusty floor tiles, working his way toward a big fancy wardrobe standing against the wall near all the kidnapped crew.

He opened the wardrobe and brought out an old-school charro outfit—jacket, chaps, silk tie, sarape, and a fancy black sombrero. Pepe held it all up in a furry paw. "Is this what he was wearing the night he met you?" he asked La Llorona.

The legendary ghoul gasped in shock. Which, by the way, was a big shock to me, because you'd never think that something as scary as her could be—well, *shocked*. Especially not by some old and probably funky-smelling threads.

"¡Sí!" she cried. "That's what he was wearing!"

It was enough evidence to make Phineas drop the act.

"Oh, all right, all right. It's true! It was me! I did a deep dive into her legend and the wardrobe of her era, and once I was in costume, I *became* her cheating husband! It was a metamorphosis! His own mother wouldn't have known the difference!"

La Llorona hissed and bared a mouthful of ghostly teeth. "¡Me mentiste! You lied to me! I should haunt you for a thousand years for this treachery!" But suddenly, she seemed to pull herself together. "But I won't! I'm leaving this terrible world behind me now that I've found my two angelitos . . ." She took her kids' hands in hers, and together the ghostly family disappeared right through the solid brick wall, never to be seen again.

CHAPTER 33

"It's over, Phineas," I said, pushing slowly to my feet while next to me, Carter did the wet-dog shake, splashing me everywhere. "We're closing the final act."

Phineas had sort of crept his way over to us—I'd thought it was because he was scared stiff of Pepe and his furry compadres, but I was wrong. "Think again, swine!" he snapped.

Next thing I knew, there was a metallic swishing sound and a flash of steel as the method actor extraordinaire drew a sword from a scabbard on his hip.

I hadn't noticed his sword or the scabbard until just now, but you could tell from the wicked gleam of the blade that it was no silly prop sword. It was legit.

Now, in case you didn't know, Carter has only

two fears in this world. One is truffles—yeah, those ganache-filled chocolate treats (long story). The other is anything sharp and pointy.

Translation: suddenly, our ferocious seven-foot-tall bodyguard didn't look so big or so ferocious.

Yeah, that's my bodyguard using my body to guard his now.

"Any of you two-legged bats move a muscle, and I skewer the brats!" he warned the chupacabras. "Back off! BACK OFF, ALL OF YOU!"

The chupacabras slowly retreated into the shadows along the side wall, snarling and growling at

Phineas, but knowing they had to take this dude very seriously.

He glanced down at his watch. "In exactly eight minutes, the cell phone in my pocket is going to ring, and that will be my driver calling to let me know that he's arrived with my limo. At that point, the four of you are going to march out of this studio with me, on your absolutely *best* behavior, or I'm going to relieve you all of your most important body part. Is that clear?"

"Crystal!" squeaked Ernie. "Just don't hurt my tummy, okay?"

"I was talking about your heads, you cretin!" Phineas raged, slashing at the air with his sword.

Trying to play it action-hero cool, I said to Phineas, "A sword? Seriously? You might want to check your calendar, Peter Pan, 'cause we're in the twenty-first century."

The hint of a mean smile touched his thin lips. "You jest, but indeed it was during my legendary portrayal of Peter Pan in the Gershwin Theatre, many moons ago, when my love for the saber was first kindled. Modern weapons are so vulgar and crass. Nothing fells an enemy quite as elegantly as a sword!"

And he whipped it glitteringly through the air in big, slashing Xs.

He wasn't bad at it, either. Show-off.

Phineas's cold eyes snapped to Liza. "Now, kindly return my memento, and I promise to make your final curtain calls as painless as humanly possible."

Liza held the little golden head out toward him. "I'll give it back," she said. "But first I just want to know how it ended up in the janitor's vacuum cleaner. I mean, every other part of your plan was executed to perfection. This was your one mistake. The only obvious clue you left behind. What happened?"

"I will tell you," Phineas said coldly, "only because I cannot refuse a defeated foe's last request. See, the venerable screenwriter Robert Villegas managed to discover my true identity. Quite accidentally, of course. He came into my trailer, uninvited and unexpected. He saw me out of costume and, given my unmistakable face, recognized me instantly. Before I could nab him, he fled from my trailer and apparently tried to contact the police, but was unable because of the terrible reception in this stage. Then, perhaps beginning to doubt his own eyes, he returned to my trailer for a second look, just to be sure. That was Robert Villegas's final error in judgment. His first had been many years ago, thinking his lines were gospel and my ad-libbing unsuited for the lips of Gaston LeBrave. I would not, however, make the same mistake twice. I seized the opportunity and captured Robert, though in the struggle, the Oscar's head—which I have long treasured as my personal talisman—must've slipped from my pocket." Phineas gave a careless shrug. "In any event, it was only a trivial oversight. I'm not upset about it. Let me get my hands dirty for once. Play the ruffian! I got so caught up in the moment, in fact, I even let out my very best wailing shriek!"

"I don't get it, dude," I said. "All this because you got fired from one movie?"

"*The Desert Rose* wasn't *a* movie, it was THE movie!" he roared at me. "The cinematic role of a lifetime! The role my ENTIRE career had been leading up to! You four brats have no idea the kind of sacrifices a *true* actor makes for his craft! I spent an entire fifteen months living in the woods, eating insects and chopping firewood so that I could truly get inside the head of Gaston LeBrave, the movie's protagonist! That's how far I was willing to go for this role. I gave it *everything*. And then that charlatan of a producer, Archie Gomez, snatched the role from me and handed it to some filthy ham! As a result, I took several *new* roles ... a lawyer, a banker, a secretary, an accountant, a film director, and so on, infiltrating and systematically dismantling all of Señor Gomez's business ventures, one by one. To this end, I have dedicated the last six years of my life. And now, with the annihilation of his production company, I deliver the final death blow!"

Then, as if to drive home the point of his little monologue, he drove the point of his sword straight through a wax apple hanging from an overhead branch.

"I heard you were a total diva on set," I said. "Making up your own lines and stuff. Seems kind of petty."

"It's called *improvisation*, you vermin!" he snapped. "Every great actor does it! Understandably, your puny mind cannot comprehend this, but the moment I stepped foot on set, I *became* Gaston LeBrave! I was him from the toes up! I knew better than *any* screenwriter what he would say and what he wouldn't. The script was all wrong! Wrong! And *I* was right!"

Okay, so I'd *definitely* steered this conversation down the wrong side street, because the guy's chest was now huffing and puffing with rage, the veins in his neck standing out like steel cables, and his eyes blazing with a pale blue fury. In other words, I'd driven this guy right off a cliff and we were about to get carved up worse than a Thanksgiving Day turkey!

Enough of this pointless blabbering! Now it's time for the four of you to make your final curtain call!

CHAPTER 34

I had just opened my mouth to say my prayers when—*CRAAASSHHHH!*

The side wall of the stage exploded as something came slamming through it in a shower of bricks and plaster. I caught a glimpse of a huge shiny rectangle of metal—a car fender!—and then I watched that fender play bumper cars with everybody's *least* favorite revenge-obsessed movie star. KAPOWWW! The dude went flying. You'd think he'd sprouted wings. A stack of junky cardboard boxes broke his fall, but he still smacked his head hard enough to put him out colder than a baby after feeding time.

A heartbeat later, my grandparents and mom jumped out of the car. "Jorge!" my mom cried.

"Mom! Grandma! Grandpa! What are you doing here?" I shouted.

"That's what we're here to ask *you*, mister!" my mom snapped, stomping over to where Liza, Ernie, Carter, and I were all still sort of huddled together in fear and shock. "How could you lie to your grandma like that and come all the way back to L.A. without first telling me?! That was *extremely* irresponsible of you, Jorge!" At that point, I was pretty sure she was going to grab me by the ear and drag me back to the car, totally embarrassing me in front of my friends, but she didn't.

Instead, she wrapped me up in a huge hug and kissed me on top of the head and told me how bad she'd missed me and how much she loved me. I told her how much I loved her, too, and that I was sorry, which I kind of was. We really could've gotten hurt coming out here. We just almost *had* ...

"And *you*," my mom said, whirling around to face my dear old granny. "Don't think I'm done with you! How could you let him have come all the way out here alone?!"

"What's the big deal?" my abuela shot back. "He came with his monster friend. I knew Carter would take care of him. Besides, I needed some time off from looking after the kid."

I blinked, surprised. "Hold up. So you knew the whole camp thing was made up?" I asked Paz.

"Of course I knew, ¡cabezón! I got the info out of your big-mouthed furry friend. But it would get you out of my hair for a couple of days, so I figured it was a win-win."

Shocked, I whirled around to face Carter. "Dude, you told her?"

He gave me a sheepish grin/shrug combo. "She scared me into tellin', Jorge..."

"*Scared you?!* Carter, she's like four feet tall, and you got FANGS!"

"Yeah, but she got dat big iron pan," he said, "and she swing it real hard."

Eh. I couldn't argue with that one. My grandma and her pan were a scary combo.

"Linda, look." Paz had come over and was now holding up Carter's long furry arm, showing off the "friendship bracelet" she'd given him before we'd left. "My GPS dog collar idea worked to perfection! I knew right where they were the whole time! Now who's the irresponsible guardian?"

"But, Mrs. Lopez, how'd you know we were in trouble?" asked Liza with a confused frown. My grandma looked at her with an even *more* confused frown.

"*Trouble?* You all are in trouble? It better not be money trouble, 'cause I'm not spending one more penny helpin' out Mr. Potato Head over here!" (Yeah, she was talking about me.)

"Jorge's grandfather called me yesterday evening," my mom explained to Liza. "He told me everything and said they were on their way over to L.A. to find Jorge."

"Yeah, the big tattletale!" my abuela grumbled. "I didn't even want to come, but he guilt-tripped me into it. Saying I was being irresponsible letting four kids run around California *all alone* and blah, blah, blah..."

"Your grandma has a tendency to watch her GPS when she's driving," said my grandpa, "and not the road. As a result, we end up *inside* places instead of out *in front* of them."

"Jorge, why did you run away to L.A.?" my mom asked me anxiously as she gently stroked the hair out of my face. "We talked about this, baby. I thought we agreed that you were going to be staying with your abuelos for a little while."

"Mom, I *didn't* run away," I tried to explain. "I came here to help some friends."

Going over to the long, thick curtain, I yanked it back, revealing the kidnapped cast and crew still sitting, bound and gagged, at their desks.

"And *him*," I said, walking over to my dad and removing his gag.

My mom's eyes widened to the size of softballs, and I hadn't heard her sound so shocked since I'd accidentally swallowed a tadpole in second grade. "*Manny?*"

"Hey, what's that deadbeat doing here?!" my grandma snapped.

"Linda? What are you doing here?" whispered Manny, staring back at my mom with eyes that were almost as big and round as hers, while I undid the ropes around his wrists.

"I am certainly not here to answer any questions from *you*," my mom told him. "*That* I will tell you!" I'd never seen her go from zero to furious that fast. She would've made a Ferrari blush. Then, in a warning mama-bear growl, "And I *told you* to stay away from Jorge!"

If possible, Manny looked even more shocked. He turned to me. "Wait. He's Jorge? *Our Jorge?*" You could hardly even hear him now. "I mean . . . you . . . you're *my son?*"

"'Son' is a strong word for a loser like you," my granny chipped in. "Try 'offspring,' maybe."

"Paz, por favor . . ." my grandpa grumbled.

But my eyes never left Manny's. "Hiya, Pops," I said with a little wave. My heart was beating so hard it actually hurt me. It felt like a subwoofer in my chest, and I wondered if anybody else could hear it, too. "Now, I've got to ask *you* a question." It was the question I'd been waiting to ask all my life. I wasn't sure I could get the words out, but I went for it, anyway. And to my huge surprise, they just sort of came rolling right out: "Why'd you leave us?"

It was like the sixty-four-thousand-dollar question on *Who Wants to Be a Millionaire*. The whole audience, everybody around us, went dead quiet.

Only for me, this was the *million*-dollar question. I just had to know.

After a long, staring second, Manny's eyes dropped to his hands and he said in a small, embarrassed voice, "It's going to sound silly. But when your mom got pregnant, I got scared."

"Ha! That's original!" shouted Paz. "I wish it would've been *you* who'd gotten pregnant so you could've felt some *real* fear!"

Manny did his best to ignore that. "I know it's a sorry excuse," he told me, "but it's the truth. I got scared. So I ran away." His shoulders shrugged weakly. "Like I've always done when I get scared."

"It's because deep down inside you're nothing but a scared little boy!" shouted my sweet old granny.

"Paz, *please...*" my grandpa whispered.

Tears were trickling down my cheeks now. I hadn't realized it, but they were. "Why didn't you ever come see me?" I said angrily, shakily, my eyes still locked on Manny's. My throat felt so tight I thought I was going to choke even as I spoke. "Why not even once, huh? Not even one time?"

Tears were swimming in Manny's eyes, too. "A lot of reasons," he whispered, glancing quickly away again. "None of them any good."

"That's the first true thing that's ever come out of that man's mouth!" I heard Paz say.

Suddenly, Manny looked up at me again. His face was open, earnest. "It wasn't all my fault, though, Jorge. I *wanted* to come see you. It wasn't just me."

"No, it was *my* fault, right?" My mom now. Sounding angry. Sounding frustrated. "I forgot. This used to be our favorite game, right, Manny? We used to play it all the time. The How-Is-It-Linda's-Fault game. I'm out of practice, but you seem like you've kept up your skills."

My dad: "You know you wouldn't have let me see him. Or *you*."

My mom: "Of course not! So you could break our hearts all over again?"

Dad: "You weren't the only one hurting, Linda. It's not always about you!"

Mom: "You're right! It was *never* about me when we were together. It was always about you, Manny. What *you* wanted. What *you* needed. Everybody else came a distant second!"

Back and forth, back and forth. They wouldn't quit. It was hurting my ears. It was hurting my heart. I felt like I'd been hearing them fight all my life, even though this was the first time I'd ever seen them in the same room together. It was awful, and I could feel myself shrinking, smaller and smaller, until I wasn't even sure anyone would hear me if I started to scream.

"¡Ya basta!" shouted a voice. "Stop it!"

I turned. It was Carter. He was almost crying, too. I saw his big brown owl eyes, shiny with tears, move from my mom to my dad, then back again. "You two loved each other once," he said to them in his small, shy voice. "Even if only for a little while. And out of dat love came something amazing. Something beautiful... *Jorge!* What is dere to fight about?"

Then the big lovable furball came over and put his arms around me and held me close to his bony, bumpy side. "Jorge is my favorite person in da whole wide world. Thank you for making him," he told my mom and dad, and I honestly didn't know what to say. I was touched.

My mom said shyly, "Well, I am grateful to him for bringing Jorge into my life..."

My dad, also shyly, echoed, "He's a great kid. And that's all thanks to his mom."

Even my abuela looked kind of touched. "Well, I don't know about *beautiful*," she said, glancing back over at the big guy. "But the bloodsucker makes a fair point. I think I speak for everyone when I say that Jorge probably isn't the worst thing that ever happened to us..."

"Wow. Thanks, Grandma." I clapped back with an eye roll, but I'm pretty sure that was just her way of saying *I love you*.

My abuela smiled at me. "You know I love ya, kid.

If I didn't, you think I'd keep wrecking my flyest ride?"

Only, like most movie villains, Phineas Alcaraz was almost impossible to get rid of. I had forgotten all about our chupacabra buddies, but just then Pepe leapt out of the shadows, shouting, "Jorge, watch out!"

But it was too late. Because Phineas Alcaraz had come crawling out of the rubble, sword in hand. The next thing I knew, his rough hands grabbed me from behind, and I felt the kiss of cold steel against my neck!

CHAPTER 35

"Touching moment!" the kidnapping thespian hissed close by my ear. "You've given me plenty of material to draw from for my next family drama. But I'm afraid it is now time to draw the curtains on this most tender of reunions. Nobody move—human or fanged—or I cut the boy!"

But my grandma was already on the move, running back to her car. She dug around in the glove compartment, cheered when she found something, and then came racing back over with a napkin and pen in her hands.

"Lady, did you not hear me?" asked Phineas, clearly annoyed by her.

"Oh, I heard you," said Granny Dearest. "I've just always wanted your autograph, and I thought exposing Jorge to a little danger was way worth it! Can you make it out to Sassy P?"

My eyebrows screwed up in confusion. "Who's Sassy P?"

"That's what all the boys in the barrio used to call me when I was way younger and just a bit more beautiful. I was *pretty* popular in those days, let me tell ya."

My gag reflex kicked in pretty hard right about then. "Gross."

Phineas, though, ever the pro, signed her autograph one-handed so he could keep the blade of the sword nice and tight against my throat. Sweetheart, that guy.

Paz couldn't have been more excited. "Yes!" she said, folding the napkin up neatly and slipping it into her pocket. "I knew we'd meet somebody famous out here!"

"Let my son go!" my mother ordered Phineas, giving him the sort of fiery-eyed look that would've sent even a hungry lion running back into the bush for cover. "I'm going to count to five..."

"Don't let her fool you!" I told Phineas. "She never gets all the way to five. Once she hits three, you're done! You better let me go already just to be on the safe side!"

"Silence!" Phineas snapped at me.

"Let him go already!" Carter and Ernie both pitched in.

"I hate to point out the obvious," Liza told the world's most annoying actor, "but you're outnumbered. And by *a lot*. I don't even think Captain Kirk could handle these odds."

"Actually, Kirk's beaten worse odds," Ernie chimed in, earning himself a swift elbow to the ribs, courtesy of Liza.

Phineas sniffed. "Don't dare compare me to that insipid character! He couldn't find his way out of a paper bag without his vastly more intelligent crew. Whereas I—"

That's when two things happened at nearly the exact same time. First, I heard the familiar boomerang-like whistle of an incoming chancla screaming our way.

Next, the missile-like sandal hit the sword-wielding thespian square between the eyes, knocking him out cold.

It was a pinpoint-accurate throw! Not even the

Hall of Fame pitcher Sandy Koufax could've pulled it off! Only my abuelita!

"Nobody messes with my grandson," Paz said to the snoozing Phineas. "But thanks for the autograph."

With Phineas down for the count, the rest of the chupacabras came out of hiding. I heard a bunch of frightened mumbling and gasps from the kidnapped crew, but surprise, surprise, my mom was totally chill about them. And seeing as she'd grown up on my grandparents' farm, my guess was that she'd run across her fair share of these lovable fang-toothed Chewbaccas.

As Carter and I gave each other the biggest *Phew!* looks of all time, Ernie came over to give me some skin. "Glad you didn't *lose your head* over the situation," he said, grinning.

"Ha, yeah. I'm not going to lie, though—it was an awfully *close shave*." It wasn't my best one-liner ever. But I still got a laugh out of Ernie and the big guy.

"What a couple of cheeseballs," Liza snorted. She'd come over to join the Hug-O-Rama, slinging her arms around the three of us. "Everybody alive?"

I showed her my pearly whites. "Close enough."

My mom asked, "Anybody hurt?"

Ernie shook his head. "Doesn't look like it."

Liza grinned around at us. "Looks like we did it again, huh?"

I laughed. "And this time, by the hair of our *chinny-chin-chins*."

"Hey, I don't want to brag or anything," said Ernie. "But I think the four of us are now four-and-oh against kidnappers, arsonists, and just general bad actors."

"I see what you did there." I grinned at him.

"Think we should go into business?" asked Liza.

"Why not?" I said. "Open a sleuthing office here in L.A. It's a cool town, isn't it?"

Ernie nodded. "A very cool town. It's the birthplace of Captain Kirk."

"You know, my dad *has* been wanting to expand his shop into California," Liza said. "Maybe we could rent a two-story studio. Butcher's shop on the bottom, sleuth office upstairs."

I glanced over at the big guy. "What do you say, Carter? You're a world-famous *gazillionaire* now. Can you pony up the dough for us to open our own detective office here?"

"But I don't got any ponies, Jorge," Carter said seriously. "And I already made cookies last night with all the rest of the dough in the fridge. But I still got a pile of those little paper checks dat the mailman brings. You think you can use dat instead?"

"I think that should cover it," Liza told him, and we all started cracking up.

"The four of you better count me in on that," said Paz. She came over, waving around her other sandal. "You're gonna need some toughness and street cred in your crew. Besides, who do you know that can sling a chancla like your granny?"

Nobody, I thought, giving my abuelita a hug. *Nobody at all.*

Just then Pepe's grandpa came over to have a chat. He had a sad look on his face, which sort of confused me, because everything was cool now. He said, "Carter, I have some bad news. Remember when I said that I could find your family? I'm sorry, but I could not."

And now the big guy was frowning, a frown so deep and sad that it honestly broke my heart. Broke it in two. Man, and I told him not to get his hopes up! "Is okay, Carlos," Carter whispered, eyes dropping to his furry feet. "You tried you best."

Pepe's grandpa was nodding. "We did. My very best. But in the end, it was them who found *us*..."

And suddenly another chupacabra leapt through the big square hole in the wall. In her arms were two baby chupacabras—a pair of mini-Carters, it looked like—and she was staring at the big guy with two huge owl eyes swimming behind walls of shiny lágrimas.

"Mamá?" Carter gasped.

The chupacabra's voice trembled as she said, "Carter?"

"*¡MAMÁ!*" And they both flew toward each other, coming together in an enormous fur-covered bear hug. Of course, there were some tears, and a lot of squeezing, and even a few laughs. It was totally heartwarming. "Mamá, how did you find me?" Carter whispered through tears.

"It was kind of hard not to. We saw you in a commercial on TV and I said, 'That's my Carter!' So I went to find Carlos, because I knew he could find *you*."

I gaped. "Dude, you have a TV commercial, too?"

Carter beamed at me. "Uh-huh. It's toothpaste commercial. My line goes, 'It keeps my fangs sparkly clean!' And then I grin. Like dis." He showed me. It was pretty scary.

It didn't take a genius to figure out that my mom and dad weren't ever going to be best buds again. But I was cool with that. Sometimes that's just how life works out.

However, they both promised they were going to do everything they could to be *my* best buds, and that's really all that matters in the end.

In case you're wondering, we did end up saving Mr. Gomez's production company. With Phineas behind bars, Mr. Gomez was able to hire a director who was more interested in serving up a finished movie than a cold platter of revenge.

Mr. Gomez also made a brilliant move and gave the lead role in the movie to Carter, pretty much guaranteeing it would be a box office smash.

His production company went from nearly bankrupt to rolling in moola, almost overnight! Which, of course, saved Mr. Gomez's land, and Pepe and his chupacabra clan's ancestral home.

I really can't explain how good it feels to do something nice for others. If I learned anything over the last few months, it's that one act of compassion can change a thousand lives.

I like to think of it as the butterfly effect of kindness.

And it's a pretty powerful thing.

Anyway, I guess you could say that we'd all gotten our Hollywood ending. Though that might not have been truer for anyone than it was for Carter...

SINK YOUR FANGS INTO ALL FOUR CHUPACARTER ADVENTURES!

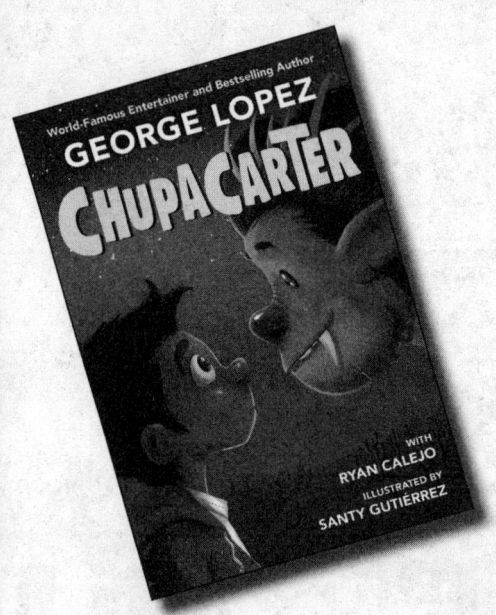

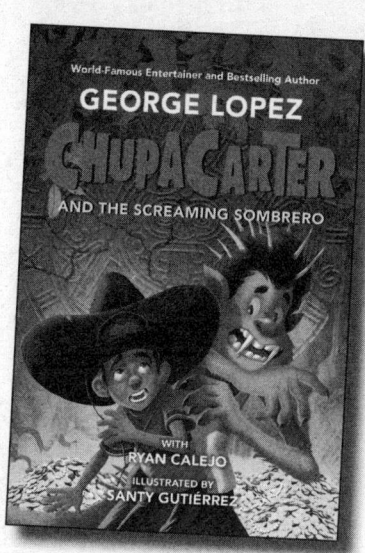

AVAILABLE NOW!

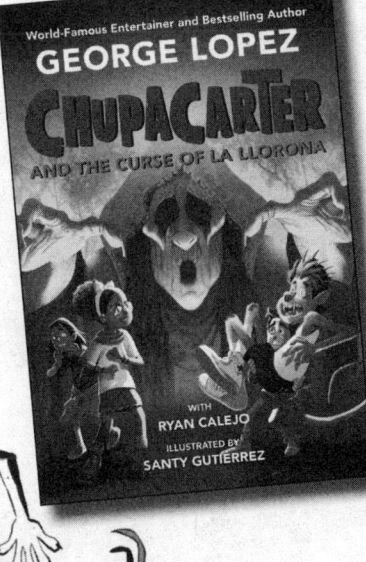

GEORGE LOPEZ's multifaceted career encompasses television, film, stand-up comedy, and late-night programs. He currently stars in and executive produces the NBC sitcom *Lopez vs. Lopez* and can also be seen in his Netflix original comedy special, *We'll Do It for Half*. His autobiography *Why You Crying?* was a *New York Times* bestseller. He has received a star on the Hollywood Walk of Fame and was named one of the 25 Most Influential Hispanics in America by *TIME* and one of the Top Ten Favorite Television Personalities by the Harris Poll. ChupaCarter is his first series for children.

Visit him online at **GeorgeLopez.com**.

RYAN CALEJO is an award-winning author born and raised in south Florida. His critically acclaimed Charlie Hernández series has been featured on half a dozen state reading lists and is a two-time gold medal winner of the Florida Book Awards.

Follow him on social media
@RyanCalejo.

SANTY GUTIÉRREZ grew up in Vigo and now lives in Corunna (La Coruña), both seaside cities in Spain. In his career, he has won acclaim as the Best Spanish Young Editorial Cartoonist and Best Galician Caricaturist, and he founded the BAOBAB Studio Artists' Collective. His wife and son are his personal inspirations.

Follow him on Instagram
@SantyGutierrez_Art.